Also by A. S. Byatt

FICTION
The Shadow of the Sun
The Game
The Virgin in the Garden
Still Life
Sugar and Other Stories
Possession: A Romance
Angels and Insects
The Matisse Stories
The Djinn in the Nightingale's Eye
Babel Tower

CRITICISM
Degrees of Freedom: The Novels of Iris Murdoch
Unruly Times: Wordsworth and Coleridge
Passions of the Mind: Selected Writings
Imagining Characters (*with Ignês Sodré*)

All rights reserved under International and Pan-American
Copyright Conventions. Published in the United States
by Random House, Inc., New York.

RANDOM HOUSE and colophon are registered trademarks
of Random House, Inc.

This work was originally published in Great Britain by
Chatto & Windus Limited, London, a division
of Random House UK, in 1998.

"Baglady" appeared in the *Daily Telegraph*, and "A Lamia in the
Cévennes" in *The Atlantic Monthly*, © 1995; "Jael" in
The Guardian, © 1997; "Christ in the House of Martha and Mary" on
Word Pictures, BBC Radio 3, and in *You* magazine, *Mail on Sunday*,
and "Crocodile Tears" in *The Paris Review*, © 1998.

Library of Congress Cataloging-in-Publication Data
Byatt, A. S. (Antonia Susan).
Elementals : stories of fire and ice / A. S. Byatt.
p.   cm.
ISBN 0-375-50250-5
1. Polarity—Fiction.   I. Title.
PR6052.Y2E44   1999   823'.914—dc21   99-10627

Random House website address: www.atrandom.com
Printed in the United States of America on acid-free paper
2 4 6 8 9 7 5 3

First U.S. Edition

Elementals

Stories of Fire and Ice

A. S. BYATT

RANDOM HOUSE

NEW YORK

For Claus Bech

Acknowledgements

I am grateful to my Norwegian editor, Birgit Bjerck, for telling me about the one tree, and for information about Peter Gynt. I am also grateful to David Perry for commissioning the ekphrastic tale about Velasquez. My husband, Peter, gave me a central idea about Jael, and Helen Langdon found several images of Jael that were most illuminating. I am, as always, grateful to Jenny Uglow, best of readers, for patience and inspiration. And also, as always, to Gill Marsden for order out of chaos.

The author and publishers are grateful for permission to reproduce the following illustrations:

Nîmes crocodile: from *The Crocodile of Nîmes* by W. Froehner, Paris, 1872; *Sirène* by Henri Matisse: from Ronsard's *Florilège des Amours*. Collection Musée Matisse. © Succession H. Matisse/DACS 1999; *Façon de Venise* goblet: © Sotheby's Picture Library; *Jael and Sisera*, School of Rembrandt: Kent County Council, from the Kent Master Collection; detail from *Kitchen Scene with Christ in the House of Martha and Mary* by Velázquez: © National Gallery, London.

Contents

Crocodile Tears

Le Crocodile de Nîmes

Crocodile Tears

Patches of time can be recalled under hypnosis. Not only suppressed terrors but those flickering frames of the continuum that, even at the time, seem certain to be forgotten, pleasantly doomed to nonentity. So they have sunk into our brains after all, are part of us. Patches of time is a mild metaphor, mixing time and space, mildly appropriate in art galleries, where time is difficult to deal with. How do you decide when to stop looking at something? It is not like a book, page after page, page after page, end. You give it your attention, or you don't. The Nimmos spent their Sundays in those art galleries that had the common sense to open on that dead day. Not the great state galleries, but little ones, where some bright object or image might be collected. They liked buying things, they liked simply looking, they were happily married and harmonious in their stares, on the whole. They engaged a patch of paint and abandoned it, usually

3

simultaneously, they lingered in the same places, considering the same things. Some they remembered, some they forgot, some they carried away to keep.

That Sunday, they were in the Narrow House Gallery, which specialised in minor English art, drawings, prints of flowers, birds, angels, handscreen landscapes and pop art posters. It was higgledy-piggledy, with real plums in the duff, Tony Nimmo used to say. The Gallery was in Bloomsbury, in what had been an eighteenth-century private house; it went up and up, with small rooms opening off a turning stair, which was also hung with stags and sunsets, garden gates, watering cans and silver lakes with swans on. They always had a good pub lunch on these Sundays. This one was a sunny Sunday in early May, a really sunny Sunday that narrowed the eyes in the light, that warmed the skin, even through glass. Patricia ate prawn salad; she was watching her figure. Tony ate a robust beef and ham platter with pickles and onions. Then he had brandy syllabub. And two pints of Special. He was a large man, with a bald crown above fine dark hair. His face was peacefully reddened, a pale poppy flush. They were in their middle fifties. Patricia wore a butter-yellow suit, nipped in at the waist, and a bronze silk scarf. Her hair was bronze too, fanning up and out. She had good big breasts and a generous bottom, solid and lively. On the top floor of the Narrow House, they had one of their rare disagreements.

The disagreement was about a work called *The Windbreak*. It was small; about two feet long and one foot deep, framed in a deep, polished dark wooden frame, with brass nails. It was part collage, part oil painting. It was a seaside scene, an English seaside scene, with a blue-grey sea, flecked with dirty white, stretching to meet a pewter sky with livid oily blue patches. These took up the top two-thirds of the work. The beach had real sand scattered on a fawn surface, and tiny real shells and bits of seaside plastic reconstituted into tiny windmills and buckets and spades, sugar-pink, turquoise-blue, poster-red. Much of the left part of the beach was taken up with the windbreak. This was made up of painted cloth, in rainbow stripes, stretched on wooden pegs, representing stakes. There was also a coloured ball, Day-Glo orange with green stars on it. Patricia's indifferent glance slid over this object; she had seen, in other patches of time, hundreds more or less like it; she moved on to contemplate a delicate six-inch-square dandelion clock on a cobalt-blue ground. Tony, however, was taken with *The Windbreak*. He went up to it, and peered into its glass box. He stood back and stared. He smiled. Patricia, when he called her, turned back from the dandelion, and saw him smiling.

'I like this,' said Tony. 'I really like this. It isn't much.'

'You can't like that, darling. It's banal.'

'No, it's not. I can see how you might think it was. But it's not. It's just simple and it reminds you of things, of whole – of whole – oh, of all those long days of doing nothing on beaches, you know, the mixture of misery and being out in the air and sort of free – of being a child.'

'Banal, as I said.'

'*Look* at it, Pat. It's a perfectly good complete image of something important. And the colours are good – all the natural things dismal, all the man-made things shining – '

'Banal, banal.' Patricia did not know why she was so irritable. It had been a good lunch. She could even, secretly, see what the memory-box would look like to her if she had liked it, as opposed to disliking it. Tony and the unknown artist shared an emotion, shared a response to the conventional images that evoked that emotion. She didn't, or if she did, it provoked opposition.

'I like it,' said Tony. 'I'll buy it, it can go in my study, in that space by the window.'

'It's a complete waste of money. You'll go off it in no time. I don't want a thing like that in the house. Look at the dreadful predictability of those colours.'

'Don't be so snooty. It's *about* the dreadful predictability of those colours. About sad English attempts to cheer up sad English landscapes.'

'They don't have to be sad. Not the English, not the colours, not the landscapes. It's a dreadful cliché.'

'Clichés are moving.'

'I don't want it.'

'I do.'

'I can't stop you,' said Patricia, walking away,

past a green maze, past a departing galleon, past a hunt in full cry. She was upset; the good Sunday was threatened by Tony's bad taste. She turned round to tell him that it didn't really matter, that of course he should buy the windbreak if he wanted it, and found that she was alone in the upper room. She could hear his heavy tread winding down the stairwell. She would make it up later. Leave a space, make it up later. She turned back to the walls – a blown sheep on moorland, a huge black bull, staring furiously out of the canvas, a fragile bunch of teasels. Later all this would come back, without hypnosis.

It was perhaps half an hour before she went downstairs. She was wearing high-heeled sandals, so she went very carefully round the turns of the stairs, holding on to the banister. There was a noise downstairs, of doors, of voices; she could hear no words, but she could hear agitation. There were thuds, there was hurry. Outside, there was a siren. Cautiously, she turned the last corner. She saw the backs of a tight group of people bending over something at the bottom of the stairs. A man in a green sweater, who had been kneeling, stood up. He was holding a stethoscope. 'Dead,' he said. 'I'm afraid. Instantly. A massive infarct, I suppose. No hope, I'm afraid.' Outside, a stretcher was being carried in from an ambulance. The group split, and stood back, and Patricia saw Tony, lying on his back, on the carpet, below a large painting of an avalanche. His red face was ivory. The doctor had closed his eyes but he did not look peaceful. His jacket and shirt were opened; the grey hairs on his chest were springy. His belly was a proud mound. His shoes were splayed. Patricia stood by the banister. The ambulance-men came in with the stretcher. As the group gathered again, Patricia walked quickly behind them, and out of the open door, into the street. She walked away, quick, quick, with her head up. She stood beside the flowing traffic on New Oxford Street. A taxi came past with a gold light in a black frame. She waved, it stopped, she got in. She gave her home address, which was in Wimbledon. The driver said something, which she did not hear. She sat, clenching both fists on her handbag. It was quick.

Inside her own house she walked from room to

room in the May light, and then went upstairs and packed a small suitcase. She was an efficient woman, and she packed for a business trip – a nightdress, cheque-books, the usual pharma-copoeia, uncrushable trousers and tunics, slippers. Washing things, make-up, lap-top, mobile phone. Universal adaptor. Passport. Then she looked round her bedroom, their bedroom, and left it. She called a taxi, and looked round the drawing-room. A few photographs smiled at her: Tony in tennis things on the bookshelf, the children twenty years ago. She turned these face down. The phone began to ring. She did not answer, and after a time, it stopped. Then it began again. The taxi came. She went out, leaving it ringing. In the taxi, she realised that she should have changed out of her sandals, and nearly burst into tears. She told the taxi-driver to go to Waterloo. At Waterloo she walked from the main station to the Eurostar ter-minal, covering her tracks perhaps, and bought a ticket to Paris. It was smooth, it was easy, there was a train in half an hour. She flowed with the crowd onto the platform, carrying her little bag, and at the top of the escalator, catching sight of her dim reflection in the train window, she nearly began to weep again because of the memorable brightness of her yellow suit.

She found some dark glasses in the pocket of her case, and leaned back in her seat, staring out at fields and hedges. She refused food, refused newspapers. She slept. She woke in the dark tunnel, in a swaying space, and for a moment did not know who or where she was, only that something had happened. Then she began to worry about money. How to have money without being traced? She had money, she was the founder and managing director of a chain of shops, Anadyomene, that specialised in bathrooms. The question was, how to have money where she was going, without being traced. She had thought about this before. Vanishing without trace was an idea that had teased her through all the happy years of her married life, her working life. The idea that it was possible to vanish, that there was nothing ineluctably necessary about her work, or her home, was a condition of her pleasure in those things.

She did not think, at this point, about who might trace her. She had a daughter, Megan, and a son,

Benjamin, Ben, Benjie, both grown-up and married, but they were not the pursuers she figured to herself.

She did not know where she was going.

They brought champagne in little tub-like tumblers, and this she accepted. She felt a light-headed pleasure in the fact that she did not know where she was going. It could be anywhere at all, anywhere at all. How many people was that ever true of? The train came out of the tunnel.

She had booked to Paris, but she got out at Lille. She bought a ticket to Nice, and climbed into a TGV, going south. It was now evening. Lille station was darkening. She remembered early versions of the imagined escape. The young bride's version, standing solitary on the heaving deck of the cross-Channel steamer, a vision complete with wake, spray, crying gulls, and the moving troughs on the surface of the salt deeps under which she had just shot, sitting in her dark glasses by her brightly lit window. The successful woman's version, the rising nose of the aircraft breaking through the white froth of cloud into clear blue and sunlight, the space of creamy-curded water-vapour, the silver purr. Anywhere, at the end of it. Anywhere, nowhere, somewhere. The train was without shock. But quick. The darkening fields flung past, unreadable indicators hissed past, the sky went turquoise, Prussian blue, indigo, rusty black in the lights of the way. She slept. She dreamed, and when she woke, remembered that she had dreamed something she didn't want to remember. Her mind ran loose and nauseous, for a moment, and then she began to worry about credit cards, about whether they could or would trace credit cards. The world was small now, which was good, you could move in it with ease. But everything was linked to every other thing, and that wasn't good.

She got out at Avignon, several hours later, and took a train to Montpellier and Barcelona. Shortly after Avignon, the train stopped at Nîmes, and there she got out, it was perhaps the coincidence, the almost coincidence, of the names, Nîmes, Nimmo, that decided her. It wasn't a city she knew anything about. No one would look for her there, for that reason. She set off, in the warm southern darkness, on the high-heeled sandals in which she had come down that staircase, carrying her bag. The city has big boulevards, with plane trees, and she kept to these, walking briskly, past cafés spilling light on to dark pavements, past squares, past alleys. She followed signs to 'Jardin de la Fontaine' because that sounded like a refuge, and thus found herself outside the Hôtel Impérator Concorde, which looked, and was, large and comfortable. She went in, and booked a room. The room was curtained and shuttered. There was a large bed, with a sprigged Provençal quilt, rose and gold on cream, to match the curtains, which she pulled back, revealing tall, sun-blistered shutters and a small balcony. She looked out; below was a walled garden, full of trees, cypresses and olives, and with a fountain bubbling in golden light in a pale green-blue pool. She closed the shutters again. She found she had a semicircular bath in tawny pink, tiled round with eighteenth-century birds in pink on white glaze. She bathed, and put on her nightdress. She put out the lights and got into the large bed. She remembered briefly, the windbreak and the painted avalanche, broken trees and dislodged rocks in the arrested crush of carefully painted snow. She thought she would move money, tomorrow, out of the Jersey account, and then move it again, and then move it again. The bed was like a nest, the pillows frilled, the sheets crisp. She was afraid of not sleeping, but slept. In the morning there were bright needle-stripes of light in the shutters. When she opened them, there was the blue sky, full of pale yellow light.

Breakfast was on a terrace, sheltered by a glass wall, under a canopy. Beyond the terrace was the walled garden, with sandy paths, the bubbling fountain in its stone-rimmed pool, and a huge stone bowl overflowing with ivy-leaved geraniums, scarlet, crimson, pink. There were tall cedars and pointed yews; there was a group of silver olives, and cypresses. There was bright light, shade. It was the South. Under one of the cedars a man was writing at a folding table. He was a blond man, with a head of glittering pale curls. His long legs encompassed the little table. He wore white trousers, and a pale, blue-green linen jacket.

After breakfast Patricia went out. The hotel looked across the Quai de la Fontaine to the Jardin de la Fontaine, a landscaped eighteenth-century space, with orderly terraces, stone stairs, balustrades and carved fauns and nymphs. The houses along the quai are dignified, heavy, eighteenth-century, barred and shuttered. A wide channel of green water runs under bridges, under high plane trees, along the quai. In the distance a fountain rose and shone in a high foaming spray. Patricia turned the other way, into the narrow streets, crossing a wide boulevard. The buildings are close together, made of warm cream and gold stone, with roofs of overlapping terracotta tiles. Patricia walked. She walked between heat and shade, from cool stony courts to sudden bright squares, between heavy carved doorways into white spaces where she blinked and saw water. She saw many fountains, pouring from huge stone mouths, trickling over stones, bubbling in circular pools around bronze figures or flowing along channels. Once she saw a high sculpted crested monumental spout in the centre of a grassy place she did not cross, turning back into the small streets. She began also to notice crocodiles on bronze studs in the streets, the reptile chained to a

palm tree. The same motif was repeated in windows, on street signs. A life-sized bronze monster
crawled over the edge of a fountain in a quiet
square. She sat beside the water, under a parasol,
and ordered a coffee. She was a girl, a girl on her
first solitary trip abroad. She stared at the energetic bronze claws and curving tail, as she had
stared at the golden stones and the blue sky and
the shadows, curious and indifferent. 'Your ser-
pent of Egypt is bred now of your mud by the
operation of your sun: so is your crocodile.' He
had played Lepidus. He had wanted to play
Antony but had had to be content with Lepidus.
She remembered, with her fingertips, smoothing
artificial sun-tan into his white English tennis-
playing thighs, sinewy and pale. She remembered
the toga. She stood up again, leaving her coffee
untouched, and began to walk. She stepped
lightly, like a girl.

She shopped. She bought a pair of flat white
sandals, two pairs of linen trousers, and some
floating dresses in airy cotton, painted with dark
purple grapes on a yellow that was French, a

mustardy ochre-yellow, not like the daffodil-yellow of the bright suit she had travelled in. In the Rue de l'Aspic she found an elegant bathroom boutique and spent time in front of mirrors holding up lawn nightshirts printed with seashells, gowns sprigged with mimosa on glazed cotton, a classical column of falling white silk jersey pleats, which she bought, adding a pretty pair of golden slippers, and a honeycomb cotton robe, in aquamarine. These things gave her pleasure. She told the proprietor, an elegant young woman with dark hair and eyes, and a Roman nose, that she herself was in the business. She spoke a slow, clear, grammatical French. She had meant to be a theatre designer; they had all been theatre-mad, at university; but she had made a success of Anadyomene instead. She admired a treasure-cavern full of translucent beakers in sand-blasted glass, rosy, nacreous, powder-blue, duck-egg. She bought a gold-and-silver striped toothbrush. She went out and walked. She went back to the hotel, and ate lunch on the terrace, in the dappled garden, listening to the steady plash of the fountain. She went upstairs, arranged her purchases in cupboards and drawers, closed out the afternoon heat with the heavy shutters, and slept, curled on the counterpane. In the evening she took a bath, dressed in her new dress, and went down to dine on the terrace. There were stars and a new moon in an indigo sky. The fountain was lit from underneath, like a moving cube of glass or ice, white with blue shadows. An owl called. She had a floating candle on her table in a tall-stemmed glass cup. She saw these things with the pleasure of a post-war girl. She ate a salad of avocados and *fruits de mer*, arranged like an open flower; she ate *loup de mer*, a small silver square of fish criss-crossed with golden lines, on a bed of melting fennel; she ate red berries in a bitter chocolate cup; she drank Pouilly-Fumé. There was an excess of pleasure in the simplicity: stars, flames, water, the scent of cedars and burned fennel, the salt of olives, the juicy flakes of the fish, the gold wine, the sweet berries, the sharp chocolate, the warm air. She ate ceremoniously. There were other murmuring diners. At the other end of the terrace was the long man with the mass of blond hair. He was bent at an angle, holding a book to the light of his candle. She thought: tomorrow I will get a book. She thought slowly: getting a book was a pleasure proposed, like the purchase of the nightdress. After dinner, she went upstairs, bathed again, slowly, in the circular bath with its Provençal sprigged curtains, put on the pleated nightdress, and slept. A crocodile slipped through a dream, and went under the surface as she woke. She breakfasted on the terrace, and went out again to walk in the little streets.

The next few days she repeated. She ate, she slept, she walked, she shopped. She learned the little streets, and arrived from many narrow openings at the heavy, high pile of the Arènes. It was a closed golden cylinder, made of tiers of immense arches. She avoided it. She swung back into the narrow streets. They brought her out to the Maison Carrée, a severe cube with tall pillars, ancient in its sunny space, and to its elegant shadow, the Carré d'Art, a vanishing and beautiful series of cubes of silver metal and grey-green glass. She went into neither. In a bookshop she bought a guide to Nîmes, a town plan, a dictionary and the three Pléiade volumes of *A la recherche du temps perdu*, in French. It would be her project. She began to read in the after-lunch hush, and soon saw that her dictionary was inadequate. She returned to the bookshop, and bought their largest. Her French was not good enough to read Proust. She had to look up twenty or thirty words on each page, so that she pieced together the world of the novel in slow motion, like a jigsaw seen through thick, uneven glass, the colours and shapes hopelessly distorted, the cutting lines of the pieces the only clear image. This difficulty encouraged her to persist. She would learn good French, and then she would see Proust. She could not, she thought, sustain an interest in anything easy, a detective story or anything like that. A project was good. She bought a notebook and made a patient and lengthening list of words she couldn't understand in Proust. She sat in the walled garden of the Hôtel Impérator Concorde, under the cedars, at a wrought-iron table. Scented gum dropped on the pages of *Du côté de chez Swann*. Mosquitoes hummed like wires. Under another tree the blond man read and wrote furiously. His wrist-movements were ungainly. He rocked the table as he wrote.

She had her hair cut. Her English waves became a close shining cap. 'I am reading Proust,' she told the hairdresser, a young man in black, with the Roman nose of the Nîmois. 'That will take a very long time,' he observed. In the little guidebook, studied over coffee in the Place de l'Horloge, and the Place d'Assas, she had discovered that the ubiquitous emblem of the crocodile chained to the palm tree derived from an Augustan coin, dug up in the Renaissance, with crocodile, palm and the phrase, COL NEM, Colonia Nemausis. It was believed that Nîmes had been peopled by Augustus's legionaries, to whom he had given the land in gratitude for their victory over Antony and Cleopatra, on the Nile. François I of France had granted the city the same coat of arms, in perpetuation of the myth. The guidebook said there was no reason to believe the story. Patricia, sitting by the solid and gleaming bronze crocodile in the Place de l'Horloge, had a sudden vision of Tony in a toga, white against the white light and the white spray of the fountain. They had met through student theatre, a classical world of greasepaint and sewn sheeting and Shakespearean rhythms and clarity and ferocity. He had been Lepidus, and she had sewn and fitted the sheets. Later he had graduated to Hector in *Tiger at the Gates*, and she had made him a scarlet cloak and a crested Trojan helmet; she had fitted thonged sandals round those stalwart legs. The student theatre was a dark, hot box, peopled by flitting ghosts, too puny for their lines, but fiery, all the same. It was hard to remember, here in this square, where the stones were Roman stones, the spotlit flaring passion of that imaginary wooden box. He had called her Patra, and she had called him Antony, in those days, in secret. Large, kind Tony, through whom Shakespeare's lines spoke strong and clear, and to her. They had whispered them to each other. 'I'll set a bourn how far to be belov'd.' 'Then must you needs find out new heaven, new earth.' They had appropriated what many had appropriated. He wanted passionately to be an actor, for a year or two, and then gave up the idea, quite suddenly. So that the singing words and the brighter light of the dark box became less interesting than the complicated light of common day, so that the drama of international negotiation took over from the eloquent simplicities of love and death and power. But he could always make her smile by calling her Patra. It was a joke and not only a joke. All this she acknowledged and did not acknowledge, seeing and not seeing the lines of Hector's harness, the folds of Lepidus's toga on thin air and trickling water, beyond the dark crocodile.

She was getting thinner. She ate, but she got thinner. Other guests came and went, but she stayed. So did the blond man in the blue-green jacket. He had bought a straw hat, like the hat in which Van Gogh painted himself in the days of his madness in the fields of light around Arles. The hats were sold around the Arènes, by itinerant pedlars, woven domes ending in ragged spikes of reeds. It perched on his tough blond curls without denting them. She began to lose her sense of the businesswoman she had been, was. She walked the streets more purposefully as her sense of purpose wavered. Her French was improving rapidly. She would stop and read the local newspaper, the *Midi Libre*, which was set out on polished wooden rods, in the hotel salon. Most of the contents of this paper concerned bull-fighting. She realised slowly that she was in a bull-fighting hotel; on the walls of the bar were photographs of Hemingway and Picasso who had stayed here to admire the skills of the shining pigtailed dolls, with their braid and gilt and cockades. Later she noticed that the bar itself was called the Bar Hemingway. In the newspaper also were accounts of other kinds of combat, in which the heroes were the bulls, whose more complex rushes were rewarded with standing ovations and renderings of *Carmen*. There was almost no foreign news in this journal; what there was was North African, bombs in Algiers, tourists attacked in Egypt. And local news: school concerts, the building of cisterns, the pollution of rivers. She read it all, for the French language. One evening she sat on a sofa in the shade and worked her way through it. 'Yet another traffic accident on the road to Uzès. A man was killed by a speeding car, as he stood on the edge of a vineyard. His body was found by a cyclist. From the marks on the road it was clear that the killer had made off immediately, without stopping to offer help, or to ascertain whether his victim was dead. This is the third such accident in the region this year. The police are searching . . . '

Patricia began to weep. She thought of the unknown dead man in the road, and tears poured down her face. She moved no other muscles; she sat on the camel-coloured sofa, a dignified ageing woman, with the newspaper in her lap, and her tears splashed on to it, darkening the newsprint, the grainy dark photographed bulls, the catalogue of accidents. She could not move. She could not see. She could not imagine a moment when the tears would stop, or she would be able to stand. She suppressed all sounds; not a whiffle, not a sniff, not a whimper. Just salt water.

After a long time, certainly a very long time, she heard a voice.

'*Excusez-moi, madame, est-ce que je peux vous aider?*' She did not move. The tears ran.

He knelt at her feet, in his blue linen coat, clumsy on one knee. His French accent was clumsy, too. He changed to English, the excellent English of the Scandinavian North.

'Please forgive me, I think you need help.'

'No.' Her voice came from far away. She was

not even sure she had spoken.

'Maybe I can help you to your room? Bring you a drink, perhaps. I cannot watch – I cannot watch – I should like to help.'

'You are kind,' she said, and swayed. His words were kind, but his voice was a harsh voice, a cold voice.

'You have a great grief,' he said, still harshly. She heard it harshly.

'It doesn't matter. I must. I should.'

He put a hand under her elbow and helped her to stand.

'I know your room,' he said. 'Come. We will go there, and then I will send for a drink. What would you like? Tea? Coffee? Something stronger, for the shock? Cognac, perhaps?'

'I don't know.'

'Come.'

He supported her to the lift. He called it. It was a gold-barred lift, an old, creaking, handsome lift, like a bird-cage. He managed the doors, he held her elbow, he led her to her room, he supported her. He sat her in her armchair, with its rosy chintz frill, and looked into her swollen eyes. His face swayed before her, a white face, with ledged blond brows, a large ugly nose, blue, blue eyes in deep hollows above jutting cheekbones, a wide, thin mouth with a white-blond moustache.

'Thank you,' she said.

'Let me call for a drink. I think cognac would be best.'

She inclined her head. He used her phone, he called room service. He said:

'You have a great grief, I see.'

'My – someone – is dead.'

'Ah. I am sorry.'

She could think of no answer. She put her head back and closed her eyes. She could feel him standing at a respectful distance, watching her until the waiter knocked. He opened the door, and left with the waiter. She gulped the cognac, shuddering, and went to bed.

When she passed him at breakfast the next day, she nodded silently, acknowledging him. They did not speak, and she thought she was pleased. Over dinner that night, they smiled coolly again, from opposite ends of the terrace, inexpressive northerners. She was surprised therefore, at the end of the meal, to find him bending over her table. He wondered, he said, if she would take a *digestif* with him, in the bar. He did not mean to take up much of her time. She thought of saying no. There was an awkwardness in his acknowledgement that she might not want to speak to him. She said yes, because she owed him something for his kindness, and because there was no warmth, no pressure, in his invitation. The Bar Hemingway is a glass box, which juts from the terrace into the garden. It is full of warm, deep yellow light. On the walls are photographs of the matadors who have slept in the hotel, who have put on their embroidered waistcoats, their sculpted breeches, their long sashes, in its shuttered rooms, and gone out to dance their absurd deathly dance with cloak and sword.

They sat, side by side, looking out at the dancing blue cube of water in the dark garden. He ordered eau-de-vie Mirabelle, with ice, and she ordered the same, indifferent. He said:

'My name is Nils Isaksen. I am from Norway.'

'My name is Patricia Nimmo. I am English.'

The drinks arrived, sweet, white, glistening liquid over shattered fragments of ice. The taste was fire and air, a touch of heat, an after-space of emptiness. And the mere ghost of a fruit. She would have liked to say something banal, to keep communication to a safe minimum, and could think of nothing at all.

'I am here to write a book. I am an ethnologist. I am studying the relations between certain Norse beliefs and customs, and those in the South.'

It was a prepared little speech. He raised his glass to her. She said:

'I am on holiday.'

'I have never been able to spend an extended time in the South. It was always my dream. I, too, have lost someone, Mrs Nimmo. My wife died, after a long illness, a very long illness. I find myself – detached – and – and – well off, you would say? I wanted no longer to see Tromsø. So I work here.'

'I am sorry. About your wife. I have just lost my husband.'

'And you do not wish to speak of this. I understand. I do not intend to speak of Liv. Do you find much to interest you in Nîmes, Mrs Nimmo?'

'I somehow haven't done the things one should do. I haven't walked in the Jardin de la Fontaine. I haven't been into the Maison Carrée, or the Carré d'Art.'

'Or the Arènes?'

'Or the Arènes. I find that rather horrifying. I don't like the idea of it.'

'I don't like it either. But I go there, often. I sit there, in the sun, and think. It is a good place to think, for a man from the north who is starved of sun. The sun pours into it, like a bowl.'

'I still don't think I'll go. I find all this – ' she gestured at the photographs of bulls, matadors, Hemingway and Picasso – 'simply unpleasant. The English do.'

'You are temperate people. I, too, find it unpleasant. But it needs to be understood, I find. Why does an austere Protestant city go mad every year, for blood and death and ritual?'

He bent his pale head towards her. His pale blue eyes shone. His bony white hands were still on the table, on each side of his ice-misted glass. She said:

'I hope you do come to understand it. I shan't try.'

After this they had several more brief drinks together, in the evenings, which were getting

hotter, and heavier. Patricia did not think she liked
Nils Isaksen, and also felt that this simply did not
matter. The nerve-endings with which she had
once felt out the shape of other people's feelings
were severed or numbed. She got no further than
acknowledging to herself that he was in some way
a driven man. His reading and his writing were
extravagant, his concentration theatrical, his
covering of the paper – wrong somehow, too
much, or was it that she felt that any effort, any
energy, was too much? The pleasure was going
out of *A la recherche*, though she persisted, and her
French improved. They talked about Nîmes. He
told her things she hadn't wanted to know, hadn't
been at all anxious about, which nevertheless
changed her ideas. He told her that the city and the
water of the fountain, Fons Nemausis, were one
single thing; that this closed, walled collection of
golden houses with red-tiled roofs in a dustbowl
in the *garrigue* had been built because of the presence of the powerful source. That the god of the
town, Nemausus, was the god of the source. That
under and beyond it were gulfs, caverns, galleries
of water in the hill. That there had been a nunnery

on the hill above the fountain, around the temple of Diana, from the year 1000 to the Renaissance, whose abbesses had claimed ownership of the water. He spoke of excavations, of pagan antiquities, of religious wars of resistance to Simon de Montfort, to Louis XIV, to the Germans. He spoke of the guillotine in the Revolution, and the gibbet in the Second World War. Patricia listened, and then went shopping, or wandering. She thought, if he talked much more, or overstepped some boundary, she would have to move on. But she did not know where she would go. The weather was getting hotter. The weather-map on the television in her room showed that Nîmes was almost invariably the hottest city in France, uncooled by coastal breezes, or mountain winds, a city on a plain, absorbing heat and light. She took longer walks, for variation. She went into the Jardin de la Fontaine in the midday heat, stared into the green troubled depths, climbed the unshaded, formal staircase with its balustrades, observed a crocodile made of bronze-leaved plants in a bed of rose and white flowers, curving its tail over its back, yawning vegetably, in the dancing bright air. Nils Isaksen told her she shouldn't go out without a hat. She wanted to reply that she didn't care. She said 'I know' but did not buy a hat. Let it bake her brain, something said.

One evening Nils Isaksen broke his cautious bounds. Patricia was very tired. She had taken three eaux-de-vie Mirabelle, instead of one, and saw the cedars shifting across the too spangling stars.

'I should be happy,' said Nils Isaksen, 'if you would come with me to the ethnological museum. I should like to show you . . . '

'Oh, no.'

'I should like to show you the tombstones of the gladiators. So young. We can read the life of a city, in its monuments – '

'No, no – '

'Forgive me, I think you should make some change. I am impertinent. When I first lost Liv, I wished the whole world to be dead, too. Frozen stiff, I wished everything to be. But I exist. And you, forgive me, you exist.'

'I don't need company, Mr Isaksen. I don't need

to be – entertained. I have – I have things to do.'

Before his intervention, something had been going on, in the silence. He had spoiled it. She stared angrily at him.

'Forget I spoke, please. I am in need of speech, from time to time, but that is nothing to do with you, as I can understand.'

The dreadful thing was that her refusal had made more of an event, had brought them closer together.

The next day she decided, as she walked along the Boulevard Victor-Hugo, that she would certainly leave Nîmes. She kept in the shelter of the plane trees, like a southerner. She decided that, since she was leaving, she would do the city the courtesy of going to the Maison Carrée. Ezra Pound had said it was a structure of ideal beauty. She had read the guidebook. It was made of the local *pierre de Lens*, shining white when quarried in the *garrigue*, turning golden with time and sunlight. It was tall, high on a pedestal, with Corinthian columns ornamented with acanthus leaves, and a frieze of fruits and heads of bulls or lions. It had been the centre of the Roman forum, part of a Franciscan monastery, owned and embellished and pierced by Visigoths, Moors and monks. Staircases had been raised and razed round it. In 1576 the Duchess of Uzès had decided to transform it into a mausoleum for her dead husband, but the City Fathers had resisted. It had been a place of sacrifice according to Nils Isaksen, who had a Viking bloodthirstiness under his bloodless skin.

She climbed the high steps of the portico, and looked out between the columns at the human space around the ancient house. She could see the discreet, vanishing gleam of the Carré d'Art, across the *place*. The guidebook told her that the square house was now a museum for the city's archaeology, the endlessly unearthed Pans and nymphs, dancers and gladiators. But the guide-book was out of date. There was nothing there but red ochre paint, and a few informative placards. What do you do in a dark red space, full of stony art? Patricia walked along, around, and across. She remembered wondering when it made sense to stop looking – at a pictured dandelion, a windbreak, a frozen avalanche. She went out of the Maison Carrée in a dreamy rush, across the portico and down the steps. Between the *place* and the narrow maze of little streets runs a cobbled lane, along which cars and motorcycles run, occasionally and unexpectedly. The heat and the light dazzled her. She blinked at the dark, bright blue, at the burning white. She narrowed her eyes, and plunged forward. Several things happened. A screaming – brakes and a bystander – a grip like a claw on her wrist, twisting and dragging. She was on her knees in front of the square house, looking up at the violet form of Nils Isaksen's face above her, framed by his white-gold curls, and the spiky rim of his hat. Somewhere beyond, a dark driver, with the Nîmois nose, was making a speech of mingled reproach and regret.

'You cannot make him an accomplice – that is to say, responsible –' said Nils.

'Don't be absurd. I was dazzled.'

'You looked neither to right nor to left. I saw. You threw yourself under his wheels.'

'I did not. I could not see. The sun dazzled me, after the dark.'

'I saw you. You threw yourself.'

'And how did you come to be there?' asked Patricia, one human being to another. She stood up, wiping dust and blood from her knees and the palms of her hands like a schoolgirl. She bowed to the driver, and made a gesture of abasement with her head and arms. 'How?' she said, to Nils Isaksen.

'I was passing by. I thought I would ask you to have lunch with me. I stepped forward to do that, and you plunged. So I was able to take hold.'

'Thank you.'

They ate lunch under an ivory-coloured parasol, next to the fountain with the unmoving energetic crocodile. Patricia had quails' eggs in aspic, pale little spheres in translucent coffin-shapes of jelly, flecked with sprigs of herbs. Her palms and her knees were stinging as they had not stung since school playgrounds. The sunlight packed down, dense and brilliant. The canvas was not enough protection. Sweat ran along her upper lip, between her breasts, in the crook of her elbow. Nils Isaksen had an angry red line between his hair and his shirt collar. Blood pulsed beside his Adam's apple, ruddy where it should have been pale. He asked if she liked her aspic. He had chosen *barquettes* of *brandade de morue*. A northern fish, he said, the codfish. It seemed illicit and unnatural, made into a paste, would she say? – a purée? – with olive oil. And garlic. Excuse me, he said, you have dust on your cheeks, from your fall. May I? He touched her cheekbone with his napkin. All the same, he said, you took a plunge. I will say no more. But I was watching. You launched yourself, so to speak, from the plinth of the Maison Carrée. I would like to be able to help.

'Help,' she said. 'I don't believe in help. I believe . . .'

'Yes?'

'I believe in indifference,' said Patricia Nimmo. 'The flow of things. Anything. One thing, then another thing. Crocodile fountains. Dust. Sun. Eggs in aspic. I'm talking nonsense. The sun's moved. It's in my eyes.'

'We could change chairs. I have dark glasses. I have a hat. Please – '

They stood up. They changed places. Nils Isaksen said:

'I understand you. You will think I don't, but I think I do. To me indifference is a temptation, fatally easy. You will say that he is insensitive, he has understood *nothing*, he is a fool, everybody believes indifference is bad, but I, Patricia Nimmo, have secret wisdom, I know there is good in it. That is what you think, don't you? Whereas, Mrs Nimmo, I dare to offend you by saying I have been there, I have tried indifference, it is a good station for changing trains, then it becomes – cement. Cement. You did not launch yourself into the path of that Corvette out of indifference.'

'Out of the purest indifference. If it was a launch, it was out of indifference.'

'We are in deep.'

'Talking does no good.'

'I should like to recommend curiosity. You must take an interest. Curiosity and indifference, Mrs Nimmo, are opposites, you will say. But not truly. For both are indiscriminate. You may sit there, glass-eyed while things slip past, what did you say, eggs in aspic, crocodile fountains, the stones of this city. Or you may look with curiosity, and live. I am trying to learn this city. It is not a trivial undertaking. I am learning these stones. You are right, in part, I believe it is a matter of indifference what you learn – or rather, it is a matter of blind fate, which has a creepy way of looking like destiny. But you must be curious, you must take an interest. This is human.'

The truth was, Patricia thought, with a trace of her old wit, he looked dreadfully inhuman as he said this, staring like a gargoyle, his pale skin flaking in patches, his yellow-white curls sweat-streaked, his lips stretched with evangelical fervour. He did not create curiosity about himself, by no means.

'I take an interest in you,' he said, plucking off his dark glasses and turning a dazzled blue stare on her.

'I don't want a guardian angel, I'm afraid,' said Patricia, pushing back her chair.

'Afraid?'

'I'm sorry. I don't want, that is what I mean, I don't want – ' She stood up and walked away in the white-gold air.

Because she forgot to pay for her lunch and also because she possibly owed him her life, she went with him two days later to the museum. The building stood, almost Roman, around an inner courtyard, round whose walls, in a kind of cloister, were partly ordered rows and heaps of ancient burial stones, dignitaries, priestesses, warriors, some with effigies, portly matrons with heavy heads of hair, noseless busts in togas. Inside were more stones, much older, menhirs with strange whiskered faces and fine-fingered pointy hands, a sabre-toothed tiger, the skull of a Stone Age survivor of one trepanning who had died at the second attempt. Patricia walked briskly, and Nils walked slowly, calling her to look at choice objects. 'My favourite,' said Nils Isaksen, 'fresh with life, look here, the Roman flower-seller from Vic-le-Fesc.'

It was a white stone, carved deep.

NON VENDO NI

SI AMANTIBUS

CORONAS

He translated: 'I do not sell my crowns, except to lovers.'

'I can read Latin. Thank you.'

He took her to see the gladiators. Lucius Pompeius, net-fighter, put to combat nine times, born in Vienna, dead at 25 years, rests here. Optata, his wife, with his money, made this tomb. Colombus, myrmillon from Severus troop, 25. Sperata, his wife. Aptus, Thracian, born in Alexandria, dead at 37, buried by Optata his wife. Quintus Vettius Gracilis, a Spaniard, thrice-crowned, dead at 25. Lucius Sestius Latinus, his teacher, gave this tomb. There were only replicas in the glass case in the museum. Nils said he had hoped to be able to work on the tombs of these dead fighters. Three or four centuries, he said, of dead young men, swordsmen and net-throwers, from all over the Empire and beyond, buried now under cafés and cinemas, pâtisseries and churches. Ten or so had got turned up by accident, he said, over the centuries, out of the thousands. He hoped to find a northman, perhaps.

'Why?' asked Patricia, without curiosity.

'A buried berserker, with his amulets. It has been known.'

'He would have done better not to come here,' said Patricia. 'Hypothetically.'

43

'Do you know,' said Nils, 'that there is a theory that Valhall, in the *Grimnismal*, was based on the Roman Colosseum? Valhall was described with 640 doors – a circular place where the spirits of warriors fought daily and the dead were daily revived to feast on hydromel and the flesh of the magic boar, until the last battle, when they would go out to fight, eight hundred at a time, through the 640 doorways. The northern paradise is perhaps linked to these stone rings here. We were fighters.'

'*Tant pis*,' said Patricia. 'They died long ago. Leave them in peace.'

'Peace –' began Nils. But she had walked away from stones and bones, along a corridor, up a stair.

In a long narrow dim room, she came face to face with two stuffed bulls. They faced the doorway, balancing trim muscular bodies on delicate hoofs, pointing sharp horns, staring from liquid brown glass eyes. They had been reconstructed with anatomical intelligence, with respect. They had been killed a century apart, 'Tabenaro' in Sep-

tember 1894, 'Navarro' in 1994 at the centenary
corrida for the Granaderia Pablo Romero from
which both came. Their hides were both glossy
and dusty, Tabenaro pied, Navarro a flea-bitten
iron grey. Both skins were slashed, ripped and
stitched together like patchwork quilts, flaps
reconstructed round the wounds of *pic*, of ban-
derillas, of the sword. Behind them, along a central island trudged a dusty procession of beasts, a
sample of rejects from the Ark, some wearing
their reconstituted fur and skin, some standing
bleached and bony. A wild boar, *Sus scrofa*, and
five striped piglets; a Siberian bear; a musk bull
and calf; two differing deer; a looming derelict
moose; a young dromedary, its ears frayed to bare
holes, but its eyelashes long, tufted and curving;
behind this dusty beast the bone-cages of a giraffe
and a llama; behind these a Camarguais calf, a
very small Camarguais foal, and the skeleton of a
Camarguais horse; behind these the huge bony
head of a whale beached in 1874 at Les-Saintes-
Maries-de-la-Mer.

Round the walls of the long room were other
beasts in cages: monkeys and sloths, weasels and

beavers, spotted cats and a polar bear, orang-utan and gorilla. In one glass case were curiosities, two-headed sheep, a monster with one gentle face and two bodies trailing eight woolly legs.

And the reptiles. An amphisbaena, leathery-brown, long harmless local snakes, asps in jars. *Aspic commun. Vipère aspic, vipera aspic, Lin.* And mummies of crocodiles from Egyptian tombs, boneless, long, leathery parcels, Nîmois.

'*Le crocodile, animal sacré des anciens prêtres égyptiens, était embaumé après sa mort. On le trouve en abondance dans les tombes.*'

Nils Isaksen loomed behind her. He pointed out, to please her, that the text engraved above the roof-arch was English, from Francis Bacon, 1626.

> *Interprète et ministre de la nature*
> *L'homme ne peut la connaître*
> *Qu'autant qu'il l'observe.*

'Curiosity,' said Nils Isaksen. 'You see.'

A very large cayman was rampant on the wall behind him, not discreetly tubular like the Egyptian mummy, but clawed and brightly glazed.

'We are the only people here. The dust makes me want to sneeze. The poor beasts should have been let die decently.'

'Look at the love, in the pose of those bulls, in the stitches.'

'Love?'

'Of a sort.'

'Horrible.'

'Interesting.'

That night, as usual, they dined separately, and then drank together in the bar. Patricia was disinclined to speak. The glass angle of the bar was brightly lit in the shadowed garden. The fountain bubbled and splashed. Nils Isaksen said he had something he would like to show her. He emptied out the pockets of his blue-green linen jacket on the glass table between them. There was a scattering of stones – one or two mosaic tesserae, a fragment of the golden Lens stone, a sphere of black shiny stone, a handful of sunflower seeds, a crudely carved amulet of an iron hammer on a ring.

'I found it in an antique shop,' said Nils Isaksen.

'In a tray of little things dug up by workmen, bottles and coins and beads. I know what it is. It is Thor's hammer. It is Mjölnir. It will have come from a grave, maybe of my berserker gladiator. They were everywhere in those days, these little hammers. In marriage-beds and graves. To help the spirit on its way to Valhalla, perhaps. Or perhaps to prevent the ghost from rising to stalk the living. Maybe there are more under this pavement. Maybe.'

'Are you sure it is so old?'

'Decidedly. It is my profession.'

Patricia picked up the little dark ball. When she turned it in the candlelight it sparked with a blue fire that ran in veins and flakes in its glossy substance.

'Pretty,' she said.

'Labradorite,' said Nils Isaksen. 'A kind of feldspar.' He hesitated. 'When I put up the tombstone of my wife, Liv, I made it of a single slab of labradorite. It is a costly stone. It flashes like the Northern Lights in the land of the Northern Lights. I wrote on the stone only her name, Liv, which is to say, Life. She was my life. And her dates, because she was born, and died. It is in a small churchyard, surrounded by bare space. It is too cold for trees or bushes, mostly. I put a hammer in the grave with her, Mjölnir, as my ancestors would have done. Thor was the god of lightning. There is lightning in the labradorite.'

Patricia put the stone down, quickly. Nils Isaksen stared through the glass at the cedars and olives and flouncing water.

'In the town beyond my own, towards the Arctic Circle, there is a single tree. Those towns, you know, are as far from Oslo as Rome is. Further than Nîmes. Every winter, people wrap the tree, they shroud it against the cold. The sun does not rise for months, we live in the dark, with our shrouded tree. We imagine the south.'

He pushed his stones, his seeds, and his amulet around the glass table-top, like counters in a game.

Patricia slept deeply, at first. She woke suddenly, from a confused dream of long corridors, lined with high glass cases. She went to the window. The square pane framed the huge liquid ball of the moon's light, a full moon. The sky was spangled with stars. The light poured from the moon on to garden walls, and the great stone bowl of geraniums, fiery in daylight, now silver-rose. The air-conditioning cranked and hummed. She put her forehead on the glass. A rhythm struggled to be remembered. 'This case of that huge spirit now is cold.' She moved her lively golden toes in the soft carpet and rubbed her face on the almost-cold glass. When she opened the window, the night air was warm on her skin, though the moonlight was cold.

She ordered breakfast in her room. She slipped out early: even so, the air was like a hot bath as soon as she was beyond the shadow of the Impérator Concorde. She went to the Carré d'Art. It is a beautiful building, discreet, ghostly, absent, a space of grey glass cubes on fine matt steely pillars, taller than the Maison Carrée but deferring to it, with a kind of magnified geometrical repetition and transformation of the proportions of its elegant solidity. Inside, up the wide, steep staircase, in the calm muted light was an exhibition of the work of a German, Sigmar Polke. Patricia's attention was churning, like water boiling in a jug, a stream of rising currents, a troubled, jagged surface, a downdraught, a bubbling up. She floated from room to room, her sandalled feet soundless, her lavender muslin skirt wafting round her cool knees. Sigmar Polke is strong and witty and various. The old Patricia would have been delighted. There was a wall of images of watchtowers at the corner of barbed-wire fences. There was a room full of gay, charming images of the French Revolution. A pile of parcels, a triangle, two cubes, a diagonal, brightly spattered with tricoloured motifs, a flower, a Gallic cock, which resolved itself into the blade, ladder and basket of the guillotine. Two eighteenth-century mannikins playing in an Arcadian field with a ball which turns out to be a severed head. In another room, a blown-up drawing of Mother Holle shaking out snow from her feather-bed in the clouds. A high room full of huge, romantic, stained sheets of colour, labelled *Apparizione*. Gilded puddles, seas of cobalt and lapis, floating milky and creamy clouds and vapours, forked mountains, blue promontories, crevasses and fjords of swirling indigo, pendent rocks hanging over crimson and russet lakes with dragonish jaws or long fingers of purple and bleached bone clutching froth, veiled norns and mocking ghouls, drowning white birds and crumbling citadels. The text beside these visionary expanses emphasised vanishing and danger. Polke paints with currently discarded pigments that are poisons, orpiment, Schweinfurt green, lapis. He mixes unstable chemicals: aluminium, iron, potassium, manganese, zinc, barium, turpentine, alcohol, methanol, smoke black, sealing wax and corrosive lacquers. His surfaces shift and dislimn, the stains change, become indistinct, no shapes hold, no colours are constant. The world of these apparitions is ghastly and lovely. Patricia stared. Here were beauty and danger, flat on a wall. She said in her head, 'What shall I do? What can I do?' She stared at the falling veils of melting snow, of curdled cream. How do you decide when to stop looking at something? It is not like a book, page after page, page after page, end. How do you decide?

On the top floor of the Carré d'Art, behind the stair, is a balcony. You can step out there, and suddenly there is no smoky glass between you and the heat and the light, you can look over the city, the intricate circling of red-tiled roofs, like flattish cones. You can see the Tour Magne on the skyline. Patricia went out. The hot air was as solid as the glass. You could touch it with your finger. She floated over to the balustrade, and looked out and down at Nîmes. She leaned back in a corner, she leaned back, and stared at the dark bright blue. She was light, she was insubstantial, in her shadowy lavender dress. She leaned out. Out. The heat fizzed in her eyes and ears. Her feet left the ground, she balanced, she leaned. A hand took her wrist and dragged. Nils Isaksen grasped her other wrist for good measure. His face loomed craggy in the shadow of his Van Gogh hat. It was a very angry face. His feet were planted like lead and his knees pressed against hers as he dragged her back into the box of the balcony.

'Leave me alone.'

'How can I?'

'Very easily. Go away.'

'I think not. Not yet.'

They walked in hostile silence out of the gallery and faced each other in the hot sun on its steps.

'Please,' said Patricia, English and icy, 'just leave me alone.'

'I think I should – '

'I am going to have to leave this town because of you. Because of your interference in my life.'

'Because of my interference in your death,' said Nils Isaksen.

Patricia began to walk away, brisk and furious. She did not look behind to see what he was doing or not doing. In the Place d'Assas there is no shade. There are many modern fountains, carved in the gold stone – a huge head spewing clear water into a long narrow channel, a naked pair of youth and maiden, in bronze, catching water from a columnar structure in a pale aquamarine circular pool. Patricia came to the middle of the square and began to shake. She stumbled towards the pale blue under the dark bright sky and fell on her face towards the water, like a desert traveller in a film. Her stomach heaved. The sun clanged in the sky like a gong. Tears squeezed between her hot lids. She fell forwards to drown in two inches of warm water. And the large bony fingers of Nils Isaksen gripped again, pulling her back by her shoulders. Between the sun and her eyes he was no more than a black space, a shadow carved with spikes. He pulled her to her feet and she fell into his arms, gulping and staggering. He put his arms round her for a moment, and then transferred the Van Gogh hat from his white curls to her bronze cap. She clutched him.

'Come in,' he said. 'Out of the sun.'

They sat together in her bedroom, Patricia in the chintz chair, Nils Isaksen gawky on the pretty desk chair. The air-conditioning groaned. It was only the second time he had been in her room. He wiped her face with a cold flannel, and poured her a glass of water from the minibar. He said:

'This cannot go on.'

'It is not what you think.'

'I will tell you a story. In Norwegian it is called *Følgesvennen*. In French it is *Le Compagnon*. The Companion? It is about a young man, who dreams of a beautiful princess and when he wakes, sells all he has and sets out in search of her. And when he has walked far, and farther than far, for months, in the deep winter, he comes to a church. And outside the church is a block of ice. And in the ice is a dead man, standing upright. And when the priest comes out of the church, the young man asks him what the man is doing in the ice. And the priest replies that he is a great sinner who has been put to death, and stands there to be spat at. And it would take more money than anyone is prepared to spend on such a sinner to lay him in the ground. So he just stands there.

'When I think of you, walking up and down in the heat with no hat,' said Nils Isaksen, 'I think of the block of ice.'

'How does it go on?'

'Oh, the young man asks what the dead man's sin was. He was a butler, says the priest, who watered the wine. Not so terrible, says the young man and gives the remains of his savings for the dead man to be chipped out of the ice and decently buried. So then he has nothing and goes on his way. And that night a man comes to him, and proposes to be his servant, and the young man says he has nothing left to pay a servant. So the other says he will come for fellowship. So he comes, as a companion. And they have many adventures. They meet three old women – troll women – in three caves. Each hag invites the young man to sit in a stone chair. Each time the Companion insists that the old woman herself sits there, and she cannot refuse, and the chairs do their work, and seize them, and will not let them go. And from each old hag the Companion takes a treasure in return for the promise of her release – a sword, and a thread, and a magic hat of invisibility. But then he leaves them sitting there and breaks the bargain. I have observed,' said Nils Isaksen, 'that Norwegian heroes are particularly given to bargain-breaking. They make compacts with trolls, and think nothing of cheating.'

'It is not what you think,' said Patricia.

'What is not what I think?'

'The body in the ice. I am not the dead man. I left him.'

She told Nils Isaksen then, more or less, the story of the day in the Narrow House, and of Tony's fall, and of how she had left her life behind and come to Nîmes.

'So you see,' she finished. 'You buried your wife, under that stone, and I – I walked away. I did not see why I should not walk away.'

There was a long silence. Patricia was filled with dread, that was the word, by the uncanny aptness of the man in the ice. She told Nils Isaksen how she had fled; she expected, perhaps hoped for, judgement. But he appeared to be struck dumb by her story.

'I did not think I did wrong,' she said. 'I loved him, and he died, and that was an end. Enough of an end. But it feels wrong, terribly wrong. Not to the children, which is what you might think, leaving them to – look after – things. But to him. I left him.'

Nils sat looking out of the window.

'What happened, in the rest of the story?'

'The princess was found. In one of those castles with a fence where the skulls of past suitors are on every post. She set the young man three tasks – things to keep safe overnight, a pair of gold scissors, a ball of gold thread – which she stole back. She was bewitched, she was the lover of a troll to whom she flew every night on the back of a ram.

But the Companion made himself invisible, and followed, and seized the scissors and thread, and returned them, so in the morning the boy triumphed after all. So then she said, bring me tomorrow what I am thinking of at this moment. And he said, how can I know that? And he despaired. But the Companion followed again, he followed again, and heard her tell the ugly troll, it was his beloved head she was thinking of. So of course, the Companion decapitated the troll with the magic sword, and brought back his head. And the next day, the boy threw it down before her. And then she had to marry him. And then the spell had to be broken, with alternate baths in milk and in ashes, I remember, certainly with bathing her skin. And then she became his good wife. And the Companion went away, and after five years returned to claim his reward. So the young king gave him half of everything he had. And the Companion said, there is one thing more, born since I left. And the young king and queen brought out their son, and the young king raised his sword to divide the boy, as justice required. And the Companion held back his hand, and said, no, you owe me nothing, for I am the spirit of that man who was frozen in the block of ice. And now I may go to my rest in peace. It is a dark story, Mrs Nimmo.'

'Not altogether.'

'You are right, Mrs Nimmo. You have done wrong. To the living, and to the dead. It can be set right, I think. You can return and set it right.'

'Thank you,' said Patricia gravely. And kissed his cool, bony cheek.

She did not sleep, that night, but lay awake, still and calm, visited by hypnagogic moons and stars and waves lapping on seashores, or skies lit with flaring curtains of blue and crimson light, as though she had stepped, or fallen, into some world of mythical absolutes. When she came down in the morning, Nils Isaksen was nowhere to be seen. The hotel lobby and dining-room were full of people and life. It was the time of the corrida, and the matadors and their retinues were moving into the Impérator Concorde. Two or three photographers lounged against pillars. Dark Spanish faces nodded ceremoniously to each other, as bundles of bright cloth and weapons went into the gilded lift-cage. Patricia paid them little attention. She went out and walked through the morning, fluid and automatic, from fountain to fountain, crocodile to clocktower, Memnon's head to the naïf bronze lovers. She avoided the Arènes, as usual. In the evening the town was packed with crowds of festive Nîmois; there were bursts of music and fireworks. Patricia avoided it all. She was not in that world. She looked in the restaurant and the garden for Nils Isaksen, and he was nowhere to be seen. On the first day she thought easily that she could wait – time had become a coloured cave of light in which planets rolled like plates, and fish leaped, and toothed reptiles floated and paddled. On the second day she thought once or twice that she saw him at street-corners, but it was always other tall men in straw hats or linen jackets. She tried sitting in the garden, but that too was full of aficionados, drinking cocktails, discussing *faenas*, moving naked bronzed shoulders gracefully under the great linen parasols. On the second evening she saw Nils Isaksen, but he did not see her. He was quarrelling with the receptionist. It might have been the kind of quarrel guests have, when they have been politely requested to pay bills they cannot pay. The old Patricia, sharp as a needle, would have picked up a clue from an intonation, or a gesture. The new one, floating largely in some other dimension, registered the quarrelling with difficulty, and was about to approach Nils, to whom she needed to speak, to whom she now needed very much to speak, when she registered dimly that he was drunk. His arms and legs and head were not working together, his voice was loud and uncontrolled, his face was hot. She backed away. She went up in the lift, and lay on the bed. She ordered supper through room service, and it took a long time to come, because of the eddying tauromanic crowds in the body of the hotel. On the third evening of the corrida she made her way past the Bar Hemingway to see whether Nils was on the terrace, or alternatively whether there was a quiet table where she could sit and watch the fountain. The fountain had been turned up, perhaps in honour of the matadors. What used to be a bubbling aquamarine cube of suspended liquid was now a high spraying column, flailing a little in the air, like a turning horsetail, throwing bright droplets and white shoots of wet over the grass. At the far end of the terrace, she saw, through the real glass wall of the Bar Hemingway and the molten glass cocoon of her own consciousness, a struggle round one of the dinner tables. She could hear shouting, but no words. There was a group, like Laocoön and the serpents, one figure rising above a mass, holding above his head what seemed to be a silver buckler, and a flashing bottle. It was Nils Isaksen, his blue-green jacket stained with what could have been blood, or could have been red wine, his hair dishevelled and his mouth open in a roar, fighting off a cohort of white-aproned waiters led by the maître d'hôtel in his uniform. One or two dark Spaniards stood close, involved but not active. The mass of men swayed this way and that; the plume of water swayed this way and that in the dark garden; Nils Isaksen felled the maître d'hôtel with what Patricia could now clearly see to be a heavy silver dishcover, and was himself brought down, more or less pinioned with napkins and tablecloths, and half-led, half-carried, still struggling, into the hotel. Patricia turned to the barman, and ordered an *eau-de-vie framboise*, on ice. She sat down, inside the glass wall, and stared at the cubes of ice. The barman was explaining the disturbance to a young couple.

'Nothing serious. No, no. He criticised the *spectacle*. Not a wise thing to do in Nîmes, certainly not during the fête.'

'What displeased him?' asked the young husband, laughing, his arm round his wife's silky brown shoulder. 'The quality of the bulls, or the art of the torero?'

'The *mise à mort*,' said the barman. 'He comes out of the North, somewhere. They don't understand the death of the bulls.'

The young couple laughed again, easily.

'The culture is different in the Mediterranean,' said the barman. He saw Patricia listening, and changed the subject, easily, deftly, to the beauty of the night, the brilliance of the moon, the prevalence of shooting stars in this season.

Patricia made no attempt to find out what had happened to Nils Isaksen. She did not see him again until the Fiesta was over, and the toreadors had ceremoniously driven away in their polished old limousines, with their acolytes, their strapped trunks, their bright capes and swords.

When she saw him it was in the street, in the Rue de l'Aspic. He was looking into a shop window, his hat pushed forward over his knobbed brow, his skin spangled with unshaven gold bristles. Before she reached him, he loped away, ungainly and hurried. She followed. She followed even when he crossed to the entrance of the Arènes, bought a ticket, and went in. She waited a little, and then bought a ticket herself, and stepped into the circle.

The Arènes is not a labyrinth. It is an orderly structure of tunnels, colonnades, staircases, rising, diminishing rings of stone seats, open to the sky. At first, having gone in, Patricia walked round in the cavernous arched dark of the ground-level circuit. It smelled of musty stone, and stale urine, the urine of frightened beasts, partly masked with eau de Javel. The silence in it is numb and dumb. There were Coca-Cola machines and bins of empty champagne bottles. She made one and a half circuits in the gloom and then plunged at random under an archway and up a stair, coming out suddenly perhaps four tiers up from the sanded circular arena, with its intricate raked pattern, its red-painted wooden screens behind which men sprang or scrambled out of the way of the plunging horns. The bottom tier was very close to the ground. She had read in the guidebook that it was not thought that there had been wild-beast fighting, because the barrier was too low for safety. Only men ingeniously slaughtering men, and men ingeniously, elegantly, dancing the great beasts on their delicate hoofs, to standstill, shuddering, and the knife. Over all those centuries, people had come there to sit together, festive, and watch death.

She found it hard to see, in the light. She looked around and could see neither Nils Isaksen nor anyone else. She ducked back under her archway, made another segmented progress, climbed another stone stair, reached an upper open gallery and walked round. From the height of the heavy stone cylinder she looked down, and saw a straw hat, and a patch of innocent Norse blue-green, across the great space of the circle. So she went on, round and down, and sat on the warm stone, shaped roughly to hold her, beside him. The silence was at the same time the stony silence of monuments and the airy hot silence of midday in open spaces. It was hot, very hot, the stone was hot to touch. Below, the patterns in the swept sand were pretty and sinister. She sat still for a time, and he sat, his head in his hands, and did not move. Black birds wheeled over, high up, in their own circles.

'Nils.'

'I have nothing to say to you.'

'Are you in trouble?'

'Why should you think I am in trouble? Yes, I am in trouble. Now leave me alone, please, Mrs Nimmo.'

'I saw you fighting.'

'I was berserk.' With a certain gloomy self-approbation.

'I saw. Why?'

'Because of what you told me. And because I came here, to see the bull-fighting.'

Patricia was silent, not understanding. She

stared round the white rim of the circle. He said, into his hands, 'I thought it would be a mystery. And it was simply disgusting.'

'I could have told you that, without needing to come,' she said, taut and English.

He said something in Norwegian.

'What was that?'

' "Jeg er redd jeg var død longe førenn jeg døde." I was a dead man long before I died. Peer Gynt. The great liar. The great Norwegian folk-hero. A tissue of lies and old tales and boasting. I lied to you, Mrs Nimmo. You did not lie to me, and in the end you told me – what you told me. And I took it upon myself to be judge and confessor. But my lies are worse. What I have done is much worse.'

'I should like to know,' said Patricia, although mostly she did not want to know, and feared vaguely that the dead wife had been killed, that she was to be forced to hear something unspeakable.

'I am not an ethnologist, Mrs Nimmo. I am, or was, a junior schoolteacher. I don't know archae-ology. I never married. My wife is a lie, and the labradorite stone is a lie. All lies.'

'And the town with the one tree?'

'That is true. I lived there. I lived there with my mother and my aunt, and taught school, until I had to give up. Three years ago, my mother died. She was eighty-six. I inherited the house, and her savings.'

Patricia waited. The black birds circled.

'She had not known who I was for five years. I did everything. I washed her. I clothed her. My aunt sat and smiled and sang. Sometimes she cried. Then she too – deteriorated. I had to give up my teaching because I had two old women in wheel-chairs in one house, nodding and babbling, and shouting too, they could get very angry, they got very angry with each other . . . Then my mother died. My aunt and I buried my mother in the churchyard. The labradorite stone is a story I told myself, when I found a little piece in a shop, and it reminded me of the North.'

'And then your aunt died?'

'No. Then, Mrs Nimmo, I packed suitcases, and sold the house, and wheeled my aunt on to the train and went south to Oslo. And from there I took her to Stockholm. There is a famous clinic

69

there, a neurological clinic. I took her in there, Mrs Nimmo. I had not made any appointment. We were not particularly remarkable. The clinic was full of people like us. We met nurses in the corridors, and my aunt raised her hand to them, like a queen, and they smiled. I walked up and down, quite quickly, looking for a long line of people. There was one outside the pharmacy, everyone waits there. I put my aunt in her chair, in this queue, in the hospital corridor. She was smiling at everyone, she usually did, she was a nicer woman than my mother. Then I left, Mrs Nimmo. I had *premeditated* my act like a criminal. There is nothing in my aunt's clothing, or her handbag, to say who she is, or that she came from the North. Then I came here. By hazard, as you did, as you told me you did. I got on trains and travelled south. Europe is one, now, my movements were unremarkable. I had all my money with me. It was very premeditated, Mrs Nimmo.'

'But understandable. You were at the end – at the end – under terrible strain.'

'It was wrong. We both know that. I had a Calvinist upbringing. I burn already,' said Nils

Isaksen, gaunt and hunched under the fiery disc of the Mediterranean sun over the stone skeleton of the amphitheatre.

'I think perhaps you did the best you could – '

'I did not tell you this sorry story in order to hear you say that, Mrs Nimmo. I told it to hear it told aloud. Now, if you will excuse me, I have things to do.'

He stood.

'Will you be all right?'

'It is no concern of yours. But thank you. And yes, I shall be all right.'

He walked away, into the tunnelled arch, not looking back.

That night, she dreamed. She was in the arena, sitting where she had sat with Nils Isaksen (who had not been at dinner, or in the bar). The sky was black night, and starry, in the dream, but the sand of the arena was shining with sunlight. In its closed bright circle, two men fought. They wore unbleached white canvas or linen suits, like professional fencers, and wore also fencing masks. They had an extraordinary arsenal of weapons heaped around them. Trident, the retiarius's weighted net, short swords, long swords, heavy long swords, stilettos, poniards, mace and battle-axe. They went at each other, gracelessly and doggedly, with all these things in turn, inflicting dreadful dints, and savage thrusts, so that the canvas became crisscrossed with slits, and great gouts and gashes of blood spouted from both hidden bodies and soaked into the cloth and into the bright surrounding sand. Blood poured, too, out of the blank wire faces of the masks. First one, and then the other, were beaten to their knees, and hacked at horribly from above and below. It all took a very long slow time, and Patricia was not permitted to turn her eyes away, or leave her stony seat, or speak, or wake. When they were at a standstill, a strange thing happened. All the red blood, in which terrible strips and slivers of flesh, external and internal, floated and stuck, turned back. All the carnage flowed back, quickly, into the two men, peeling off the sand, shrinking and vanishing in stains on the buckram, so that they were again fit, pale figures, surrounded by gleaming pristine blades. And then they bowed to her, turned somersaults in the swept sand, and began all over again, hacking, thrusting, bleeding.

She noticed, in the way of dreams, that someone was sitting next to her, had perhaps been there all the time. It was Tony, looking solid and well, leaner than on that last day, and smiling. He did not speak. The bloody men had been real and inescapable. She wanted Tony to stay. She was dreadfully happy to see his living face, the wrinkles at the corner of his eyes, the kink in his left brow, the warm lips. She knew then that this very real man was not real, and felt anguish. He would go, and she would wake. She said:

'Why are they doing that?'

He smiled, as though the slaughter was normal and agreeable. He did not speak. He put a warm hand on her knee. This made her cry, and she woke.

The next day, she saw Nils Isaksen in his usual corner on the breakfast terrace. She walked straight over to him. He did not stand to greet her. She asked him if she could sit down, and he made a grudging gesture of assent. She said:

'I have decided to go back to England, Mr Isaksen. Not permanently. Just to see what they have done with him.'

'They?'

'My son and my daughter.'

'You did not speak of them.'

'They would not have wanted – to have to worry about me.'

'You have made sure they must,' said Nils Isaksen, with a touch of ice.

'I wondered,' said Patricia, 'if you would – care to – accompany me?' She was thinking in French, *voudriez-vous m'accompagner?* Her English sounded odd. He asked, unsmiling,

'What had you in mind?'

'Mr Isaksen, I must see where my husband is buried. I should not have left him. Beyond that, I don't know.'

'I have nothing in the world to do, Mrs Nimmo. I will come with you.'

Some days later, they found Tony's grave, in the churchyard near Benjie's weekend cottage, in

Suffolk. The church was one of those towered East Anglian flinty bastions. Benjie's children had been christened there. The churchyard was walled, and grassed over, with yews and cedars. Patricia had supposed that it was too early for any memorial to have been put up – there were problems, she believed, with the settlement of the soil – so she missed the grave for some time, looking for recent digging, a temporary wooden marker. It was Nils Isaksen who found Tony, all staring white, a cruciform white marble head-stone standing at one end of a white marble-bordered rectangle full of glittering white marble chips. He called to Patricia, 'Here is Nimmo,' and she came along the path, and read the incised grey writing. Anthony Piers Nimmo. His dates. Beloved father of Benjamin and Megan. There were no flowers. Patricia had brought anemones, crimson, purple, dark blue, wax-white. She stood there, holding them, and Nils Isaksen found a jam jar, and filled it at a tap by a kind of gardener's shed. Patricia put the jar of flowers carefully at the foot of the stone. She stood there, listening to an invisible blackbird and the soft wind in the branches. Nils Isaksen stood at a distance, not pretending not to be there, not ostentatiously doing something else, but at a distance. Patricia opened her handbag and took out a dark eyebrow pencil. She wrote across the top of the stone, in careful capital letters, smaller than the incised ones:

THE ODDS IS GONE

AND THERE IS NOTHING LEFT REMARKABLE

BENEATH THE VISITING MOON.

She said to Nils, who came up to read her graffito, 'When I first knew I loved him, I was terrified he would die. I would lie awake at night, muttering these lines to myself. You get drunk on unreal sadness, but I was truly afraid he would die.'

They stood together. The earth smelled strongly of mould, and humus, and the energy of decay. Patricia said:

'I hate this sort of thing. The chips, the square bed, all that. I like the earth, you know, a sort of slow vanishing. This is vulgar.'

'It has a certain splendour. It reminds me of

snow and ice and the North.'

'I should telephone Benjie and Megan. You are right, I have treated them badly. They must know I'm alive and not ill, the bank will have said . . .'

'You could send them a postcard.'

'A postcard?'

'For a beginning. You could send it from Oslo or Stockholm. Or Trondheim.'

'You are going back?'

'Not permanently. Just to find out – what became of the old lady.'

Patricia had not been quite sure until that moment that the old lady was not an invention. She stood in the green English churchyard, staring at the glittering expanse of white chips framed in a white stone square. She remembered Nîmes, like a hot blue and golden ball, containing creamy stone cylinders and cubes. She thought of the unknown North, the green fjords, the ice, the lights, the one tree. She said:

'You would like me to accompany you?'

Nils Isaksen shuffled his ungainly feet on the moist path.

'I would not take up too much of your time. But yes, I should be grateful. Then – in that case – it becomes possible.'

'Then I will come,' said Patricia Nimmo.

They walked slowly away, side by side.

A Lamia in the Cévennes

JE veux pousser par la France ma peine,
Plustost qu'un trait ne vole au decocher:
Je veux de miel mes oreilles boucher,
Pour n'ouyr plus la voix de ma Sereine.

Je veux muer mes deux yeux en fonteine,
Mon cœur en feu, ma teste en un rocher,
Mes piés en tronc, pour jamais n'approcher
De sa beauté si fierement humaine.

Sirène, Henri Matisse, 1948

A Lamia in the Cévennes

In the mid-1980s Bernard Lycett-Kean decided
that Thatcher's Britain was uninhabitable, a land of
dog-eat-dog, lung-corroding ozone and floating
money, of which there was at once far too much
and far too little. He sold his West Hampstead flat
and bought a small stone house on a Cévenol hillside. He had three rooms, and a large barn, which
he weatherproofed, using it as a studio in winter
and a storehouse in summer. He did not know how
he would take to solitude, and laid in a large
quantity of red wine, of which he drank a good
deal at first, and afterwards much less. He discovered that the effect of the air and the light and
the extremes of heat and cold were enough, indeed
too much, without alcohol. He stood on the terrace
in front of his house and battled with these things,
with mistral and tramontane and thunderbolts and
howling clouds. The Cévennes is a place of
extreme weather. There were also days of white

heat, and days of yellow heat, and days of burning blue heat. He produced some paintings of heat and light, with very little else in them, and some other paintings of the small river which ran along the foot of the steep, terraced hill on which his house stood; these were dark green and dotted with the bright blue of the kingfisher and the electric blue of the dragonflies.

These paintings he packed in his van and took to London and sold for largish sums of the despised money. He went to his own Private View and found he had lost the habit of conversation. He stared and snorted. He was a big man, a burly man, his stare seemed aggressive when it was largely baffled. His old friends were annoyed. He himself found London just as rushing and evil-smelling and unreal as he had been imagining it. He hurried back to the Cévennes. With his earnings, he built himself a swimming-pool, where once there had been a patch of baked mud and a few bushes.

It is not quite right to say he built it. It was built by the Jardinerie Émeraude, two enterprising young men, who dug and lined and carried mud and monstrous stones, and built a humming power-house full of taps and pipes and a swirling cauldron of filter-sand. The pool was blue, a swimming-pool blue, lined with a glittering tile mosaic, and with a mosaic dolphin cavorting amiably in its depths, a dark blue dolphin with a pale blue eye. It was not a boring rectangular pool, but an irregular oval triangle, hugging the contour of the terrace on which it lay. It had a white stone rim, moulded to the hand, delightful to touch when it was hot in the sun.

The two young men were surprised that Bernard wanted it blue. Blue was a little *moche*, they thought. People now were making pools steel-grey or emerald-green, or even dark wine-red. But Bernard's mind was full of blue dots now visible across the southern mountains when you travelled from Paris to Montpellier by air. It was a recalcitrant blue, a blue that asked to be painted by David Hockney and only by David Hockney. He felt something else could and must be done with that blue. It was a blue he needed to know and fight. His painting was combative painting. That blue, that amiable, non-natural aquamarine was different in the uncompromising mountains from what it was in Hollywood. There were no naked male backsides by his pool, no umbrellas, no tennis-courts. The river-water was sombre and weedy, full of little shoals of needle-fishes and their shadows, of curling water-snakes and the triangular divisions of flow around pebbles and boulders. This mild blue, here, was to be seen in *that* terrain.

He swam more and more, trying to understand the blue, which was different when it was under the nose, ahead of the eyes, over and around the sweeping hands and the flickering toes and the groin and the armpits and the hairs of his chest, which held bubbles of air for a time. His shadow in the blue moved over a pale eggshell mosaic, a darker blue, with huge paddle-shaped hands. The light changed, and with it, everything. The best days were under racing cloud, when the aquamarine took on a cool grey tone, which was then chased back, or rolled away, by the flickering gold-in-blue of yellow light in liquid. In front of his prow or chin in the brightest lights moved a mesh of hexagonal threads, flashing rainbow colours, flashing liquid silver-gilt, with a hint of molten glass; on such days liquid fire, rosy and yellow and clear, ran across the dolphin, who lent it a thread of intense blue. But the surface could be a reflective plane, with the trees hanging in it, with two white diagonals where the aluminium steps entered. The shadows of the sides were a deeper blue but not a deep blue, a blue not reflective and yet lying flatly *under* reflections. The pool was deep, for the Émeraude young men envisaged much diving. The wind changed the surface, frilled and furred it, flecked it with diamond drops, shirred it and made a witless patchwork of its plane. His own motion changed the surface – the longer he swam, the faster he swam, the more the glassy hills and valleys chopped and changed and ran back on each other.

Swimming was *volupté* – he used the French word, because of Matisse. *Luxe, calme et volupté.* Swimming was a strenuous battle with immense problems, of geometry, of chemistry, of apprehension, of style, of other colours. He put pots of petunias and geraniums near the pool. The bright hot pinks and purples were dangerous. They did something to that blue.

The stone was easy. Almost too blandly easy. He could paint chalky white and creamy sand and cool grey and paradoxical hot grey; he could understand the shadows in the high rough wall of monstrous cobblestones that bounded his land.

The problem was the sky. Swimming in one direction, he was headed towards a great rounded green mountain, thick with the bright yellow-green of dense chestnut trees, making a slightly innocent, simple arc against the sky. Whereas the other way, he swam towards crags, towards a bowl of bald crags, with a few pines and lines of dark shale. And against the green hump the blue sky was one blue, and against the bald stone another, even when for a brief few hours it was uniformly blue overhead, that rich blue, that cobalt, deep-washed blue of the South, which fought all the blues of the pool, all the green-tinged, duck-egg-tinged blues of the shifting water. But the sky had also its greenish days, and its powdery-hazed days, and its theatrical louring days, and none of these blues and whites and golds and ultramarines and faded washes harmonised in any way with the pool blues, though they all went through their changes and splendours in the same world, in which he and his shadow swam, in which he and his shadow stood in the sun and struggled to record them.

He muttered to himself. Why bother. Why does this *matter* so much. *What difference does it make to anything if I solve this blue* and just start again. I could just sit down and drink wine. I could go and be useful in a cholera-camp in Colombia or Ethiopia. *Why bother to render the transparency in solid paint or air on a bit of board?* I could *just stop*.

He could not.

He tried oil paint and acrylic, watercolour and gouache, large designs and small plain planes and complicated juxtaposed planes. He tried trapping light on thick impasto and tried also glazing his surfaces flat and glossy, like seventeenth-century Dutch or Spanish paintings of silk. One of these almost pleased him, done at night, with the lights under the water and the dark round the stone, on an oval bit of board. But then he thought it was sentimental. He tried veils of watery blues on white in watercolour, he tried Matisse-like patches of blue and petunia – pool blue, sky blue, petunia

— he tried Bonnard's mixtures of pastel and gouache.

His brain hurt, and his eyes stared, and he felt whipped by winds and dried by suns.

He was happy, in one of the ways human beings have found in which to be happy.

One day he got up as usual and as usual flung himself naked into the water to watch the dawn in the sky and the blue come out of the black and grey in the water.

There was a hissing in his ears, and a stench in his nostrils, perhaps a sulphurous stench, he was not sure; his eyes were sharp but his profession, with spirits and turpentine, had dulled his nostrils. As he moved through the sluggish surface he stirred up bubbles, which broke, foamed, frothed and crusted. He began to leave a trail of white, which reminded him of polluted rivers, of the waste-pipes of tanneries, of deserted mines. He came out rapidly and showered. He sent a fax to the Jardinerie Émeraude. What was Paradise is become the Infernal Pit. Where once I smelled lavender and salt, now I have a mephitic stench.

What have you done to my water? Undo it, undo it. I cannot coexist with these exhalations. His French was more florid than his English. I am polluted, my work is polluted, *I cannot go on.* How could the two young men be brought to recognise the extent of the insult? He paced the terrace like an angry panther. The sickly smell crept like marsh-grass over the flower-pots, through the lavender bushes. An emerald-green van drew up, with a painted swimming-pool and a painted palm tree. Every time he saw the van, he was pleased and irritated that this commercial emerald-and-blue had found an exact balance for the difficult aquamarine without admitting any difficulty.

The young men ran along the edge of the pool, peering in, their muscular legs brown under their shorts, their plimsolls padding. The sun came up over the green hill and showed the plague-stricken water-skin, ashy and suppurating. It is all OK, said the young men, this is a product we put in to fight algae, not because you *have* algae, M. Bernard, but in case algae might appear, as a precaution. It will all be exhaled in a week or two, the mousse will go, the water will clear.

'Empty the pool,' said Bernard. '*Now*. Empty it now. I will not co-exist for two weeks with this vapour. Give me back my clean salty water. *This water is my life-work*. Empty it *now*.'

'It will takes days to fill,' said one young man, with a French acceptance of Bernard's desperation. 'Also there is the question of the allocation of water, of how much you are permitted to take.'

'We could fetch it up from the river,' said the other. In French this is literally, we could draw it *in* the river, *puiser dans le ruisseau*, like fishing. 'It will be cold, ice-cold from the Source, up the mountain,' said the Émeraude young men.

'Do it,' said Bernard. 'Fill it from the river. I am an Englishman, I swim in the North Sea, I like cold water. Do it. *Now*.'

The young men ran up and down. They turned huge taps in the grey plastic pipes that debouched in the side of the mountain. The swimming-pool soughed and sighed and began, still sighing, to sink, whilst down below, on the hillside, a frothing flood spread and laughed and pranced and curled and divided and swept into the river. Bernard stalked behind the young men, admonishing them. 'Look at that froth. We are polluting the river.'

'It is only two litres. It is perfectly safe. Everyone has it in his pool, M. Bernard. It is tried and tested, it is a product for *purifying water*.' It is only you, his pleasant voice implied, who is pig-headed enough to insist on voiding it.

The pool became a pit. The mosaic sparkled a little in the sun, but it was a sad sight. It was a deep blue pit of an entirely unproblematic dull texture. Almost like a bathroom floor. The dolphin lost his movement and his fire, and his curvetting ripples, and became a stolid fish in two dimensions. Bernard peered in from the deep end and from the shallow end, and looked over the terrace wall at the hillside where froth was expiring on nettles and brambles. It took almost all day to empty and began to make sounds like a gigantic version of the bath-plug terrors of Bernard's infant dreams.

The two young men appeared carrying an immense boa-constrictor of heavy black plastic pipe, and an implement that looked like a torpedo, or a diver's oxygen pack. The mountainside was steep, and the river ran green and chuckling at its foot. Bernard stood and watched. The coil of pipe was uncoiled, the electricity was connected in his humming pumphouse, and a strange sound began, a regular boum-boum, like the beat of a giant heart, echoing off the green mountain. Water began to gush from the mouth of the pipe into the sad dry depths of his pool-pit. Where it trickled upwards, the mosaic took on a little life again, like crystals glinting.

'It will take all night to fill,' said the young men. 'But do not be afraid, even if the pool overflows, it will not come in your house, the slope is too steep, it will run away back to the river. And tomorrow we will come and regulate it and filter it and you may swim. But it will be very cold.'

'*Tant pis*,' said Bernard.

All night the black tube on the hillside wailed like a monstrous bullfrog, boum-boum, boum-boum. All night the water rose, silent and powerful. Bernard could not sleep; he paced his terrace and watched the silver line creep up the sides of the pit, watched the greenish water sway. Finally he slept, and in the morning his world was awash with river-water, and the heart-beat machine was still howling on the river-bank, boum-boum, boum-boum. He watched a small fish skid and slide across his terrace, flow over the edge and slip in a stream of water down the hillside and back into the river. Everything smelt wet and lively, with no hint of sulphur and no clear smell of purified water. His friend Raymond Potter telephoned from London to say he might come on a visit; Bernard, who could not cope with visitors, was non-committal, and tried to describe his delicious flood as a minor disaster.

'You don't want river-water,' said Raymond Potter. 'What about liver-flukes and things, and bilharzia?'

'They don't have bilharzia in the Cévennes,' said Bernard.

The Émeraude young men came and turned off the machine, which groaned, made a sipping sound and relapsed into silence. The water in the pool had a grassy depth it hadn't had. It was a lovely colour, a natural colour, a colour that harmonised with the hills, and it was not the problem Bernard was preoccupied with. It would clear, the young men assured him, once the filtration was working again.

Bernard went swimming in the green water. His body slipped into its usual movements. He looked down for his shadow and thought he saw out of the corner of his eye a swirling movement in the depths, a shadowy coiling. It would be strange, he said to himself, if there were a big snake down there, moving around. The dolphin was blue in green gloom. Bernard spread his arms and legs and floated. He heard a rippling sound of movement, turned his head, and found he was swimming alongside a yellow-green frog with a salmon patch on its cheek and another on its butt, the colour of the roes of scallops. It made vigorous thrusts with its hind legs, and vanished into the skimmer, from the mouth of which it peered out at Bernard. The underside of its throat beat, beat, cream-coloured. When it emerged, Bernard cupped his hands under its cool wet body and lifted it over the edge: it clung to his fingers with its own tiny fingers, and then went away, in long hops. Bernard went on swimming. There was still a kind of movement in the depths that was not his own.

This persisted for some days, although the young men set the filter in motion, tipped in sacks of white salt, and did indeed restore the aquamarine transparency, as promised. Now and then he saw a shadow that was not his, now and then something moved behind him; he felt the water swirl and tug. This did not alarm him, because he both believed and disbelieved his senses. He liked to imagine a snake. Bernard liked snakes. He liked the darting river-snakes, and the long silver-brown grass snakes who travelled the grasses beside the river.

Sometimes he swam at night, and it was at night that he first definitely saw the snake, only for a few moments, after he had switched on the underwater lights, which made the water look like turquoise milk. And there under the milk was something very large, something coiled in two intertwined figures of eight and like no snake he had ever seen, a velvety-black, it seemed, with long bars of crimson and peacock-eyed spots, gold, green, blue, mixed with silver moonshapes, all of which appeared to dim and brighten and breathe under the deep water. Bernard did not try to touch; he sat down cautiously and stared. He could see neither head nor tail; the form appeared to be a continuous coil like a Möbius strip. And the colours changed as he watched them: the gold and silver lit up and went out, like lamps, the eyes expanded and contracted, the bars and stripes flamed with electric vermilion and crimson and then changed to purple, to blue, to green, moving through the rainbow. He tried professionally to commit the forms and the colours to memory. He looked up for a moment at the night sky. The Plough hung very low, and the stars glittered white-gold in Orion's belt on thick midnight velvet. When he looked back, there was the pearly water, vacant.

Many men might have run roaring in terror; the courageous might have prodded with a pool-net, the extravagant might have reached for a shot-gun. What Bernard saw was a solution to his professional problem, at least a nocturnal solution. Between the night sky and the breathing, dissolving eyes and moons in the depths, the colour of the water was solved, dissolved, it became a medium to

contain a darkness spangled with living colours. He
went in and took notes in watercolour and gouache.
He went out and stared and the pool was empty.

For several days he neither saw nor felt the snake.
He tried to remember it, and to trace its markings
into his pool-paintings, which became very tentative and watery. He swam even more than usual,
invoking the creature from time to time. 'Come
back,' he said to the pleasant blue depths, to the
twisting coiling lines of rainbow light. 'Come
back, I need you.'

And then, one day, when a thunderstorm was
gathering behind the crest of the mountains, when
the sky loured and the pool was unreflective, he felt
the alien tug of the other current again, and looked
round quick, quick, to catch it. And there was a
head, urging itself sinuously through the water
beside his own, and there below his body coiled the
miraculous black velvet rope or tube with its shimmering moons and stars, its peacock eyes, its
crimson bands.

The head was a snake-head, diamond-shaped,
half the size of his own head, swarthy and scaled,

with a strange little crown of pale lights hanging above it like its own rainbow. He turned cautiously to look at it and saw that it had large eyes with fringed eyelashes, human eyes, very lustrous, very liquid, very black. He opened his mouth, swallowed water by accident, coughed. The creature watched him, and then opened its mouth, in turn, which was full of small, even, pearly human teeth. Between these protruded a flickering dark forked tongue, entirely serpentine. Bernard felt a prick of recognition. The creature sighed. It spoke. It spoke in Cévenol French, very sibilant, but comprehensible.

'I am so unhappy,' it said.

'I am sorry,' said Bernard stupidly, treading water. He felt the black coils slide against his naked legs, a tail-tip across his private parts.

'You are a very beautiful man,' said the snake in a languishing voice.

'You are a very beautiful snake,' replied Bernard courteously, watching the absurd eyelashes dip and lift.

'I am not entirely a snake. I am an enchanted spirit, a Lamia. If you will kiss my mouth, I will become a most beautiful woman, and if you will marry me, I will be eternally faithful and gain an immortal soul. I will also bring you power, and riches, and knowledge you never dreamed of. But you must have faith in me.'

Bernard turned over on his side, and floated, disentangling his brown legs from the twining coloured coils. The snake sighed.

'You do not believe me. You find my present form too loathsome to touch. I love you. I have watched you for months and I love and worship your every movement, your powerful body, your formidable brow, the movements of your hands when you paint. Never in all my thousands of years have I seen so perfect a male being. I will do anything for you – '

'Anything?'

'Oh, *anything*. Ask. Do not reject me.'

'What I want,' said Bernard, swimming towards the craggy end of the pool, with the snake stretched out behind him, 'what I want, is to be able to paint your portrait, *as you are*, for certain reasons of my own, and because I find you very beautiful – if you would consent to remain here for a little time, as a snake – with all these amazing

colours and lights – if I could paint you *in my pool*
– just for a little time – '

'And then you will kiss me, and we will be married, and I shall have an immortal soul.'

'Nobody nowadays believes in immortal souls,'
said Bernard.

'It does not matter if you believe in them or not,'
said the snake. 'You have one and it will be horribly tormented if you break your pact with me.'

Bernard did not point out that he had not made
a pact, not having answered her request yes or no.
He wanted quite desperately that she should
remain in his pool, in her present form, until he had
solved the colours, and was almost prepared for a
Faustian damnation.

There followed a few weeks of hectic activity. The
Lamia lingered agreeably in the pool, disposing
herself wherever she was asked, under or on the
water, in figures of three or six or eight or O, in
spirals and tight coils. Bernard painted and swam
and painted and swam. He swam less since he
found the Lamia's wreathing flirtatiousness
oppressive, though occasionally to encourage her,

he stroked her sleek sides, or wound her tail round his arm or his arm round her tail. He never painted her head, which he found hideous and repulsive. Bernard liked snakes but he did not like women. The Lamia with female intuition began to sense his lack of enthusiasm for this aspect of her. 'My teeth,' she told him, 'will be lovely in rosy lips, my eyes will be melting and mysterious in a human face. Kiss me, Bernard, and you will see.'

'Not yet, not yet,' said Bernard.

'I will not wait for ever,' said the Lamia.

Bernard remembered where he had, so to speak, seen her before. He looked her up one evening in Keats, and there she was, teeth, eyelashes, frecklings, streaks and bars, sapphires, greens, amethyst and rubious-argent. He had always found the teeth and eyelashes repulsive and had supposed Keats was as usual piling excess on excess. Now he decided Keats must have seen one himself, or read someone who had, and felt the same mixture of aesthetic frenzy and repulsion. Mary Douglas, the anthropologist, says that *mixed* things, neither flesh nor fowl, so to speak, always excite repulsion and prohibition. The poor Lamia was a mess, as far as her head went. Her beseeching eyes were horrible. He looked up from his reading and saw her snake-face peering sadly in at the window, her halo shimmering, her teeth shining like pearls. He saw to his locks: he was not about to be accidentally kissed in his sleep. They were each other's prisoners, he and she. He would paint his painting and think how to escape.

The painting was getting somewhere. The snake-colours were a fourth term in the equation pool>sky>mountains-trees>paint. Their movement in the aquamarines linked and divided delectably, firing the neurones in Bernard's brain to greater and greater activity, and thus causing the Lamia to become sulkier and eventually duller and less brilliant.

'I am *so sad*, Bernard. I want to be a woman.'

'You've had thousands of years already. Give me a few more days.'

'You see how kind I am, when I am in pain.'

What would have happened if Raymond Potter had not kept his word will never be known.

Bernard had quite forgotten the liver-fluke conversation and Raymond's promised, or threatened, visit. But one day he heard wheels on his track, and saw Potter's dark red BMW creeping up its slope.

'Hide,' he said to the Lamia. 'Keep still. It's a dreadful Englishman of the fee-fi-fo-fum sort; he has a shouting voice, he *makes jokes*, he smokes cigars, he's bad news, *hide*.'

The Lamia slipped underwater in a flurry of bubbles like the Milky Way.

Raymond Potter came out of the car smiling and carried in a leg of wild boar and the ingredients of a *ratatouille*, a crate of red wine, and several bottles of *eau-de-vie Poire William*.

'Brought my own provisions. Show me the stove.'

He cooked. They ate on the terrace, in the evening. Bernard did not switch on the lights in the pool and did not suggest that Raymond might swim. Raymond in fact did not like swimming; he was too fat to wish to be seen, and preferred eating and smoking. Both men drank rather a lot of red wine and then rather a lot of eau-de-vie. The smell of the mountains was laced with the smells of pork crackling and cigar smoke. Raymond peered drunkenly at Bernard's current painting. He pronounced it rather sinister, very striking, a bit weird, not quite usual, funny-coloured, a bit over the top? Looking at Bernard each time for a response and getting none, as Bernard, exhausted and a little drunk, was largely asleep. They went to bed, and Bernard woke in the night to realise he had not shut his bedroom window as he usually did; a shutter was banging. But he was unkissed and solitary; he slid back into unconsciousness.

The next morning Bernard was up first. He made coffee, he cycled to the village and bought croissants, bread and peaches, he laid the table on the terrace and poured heated milk into a blue and white jug. The pool lay flat and still, quietly and incompatibly shining at the quiet sky.

Raymond made rather a noise coming downstairs. This was because his arm was round a young woman with a great deal of hennaed black hair, who wore a garment of that see-through cheesecloth from India which is sold in every southern French market. The garment was calf-length, clinging, with little shoulder-straps and dyed in a rather musty brownish-black, scattered with little round green spots like peas. It could have been a sundress or a nightdress; it was only too easy to see that the woman wore nothing at all underneath. The black triangle of her pubic hair swayed with her hips. Her breasts were large and thrusting, that was the word that sprang to Bernard's mind. The nipples stood out in the cheesecloth.

'This is Melanie,' Raymond said, pulling out a chair for her. She flung back her hair with an actressy gesture of her hands and sat down gracefully, pulling the cheesecloth round her knees and staring down at her ankles. She had long pale hairless legs with very pretty feet. Her toenails were varnished with a pink pearly varnish. She turned them this way and that, admiring them. She wore rather a lot of very pink lipstick and smiled in a satisfied way at her own toes.

'Do you want coffee?' said Bernard to Melanie.

'She doesn't speak English,' said Raymond. He leaned over and made a guzzling, kissing noise in the hollow of her collar-bone. 'Do you, darling?'

He was obviously going to make no attempt to explain her presence. It was not even quite clear that he knew that Bernard had a right to an explanation, or that he had himself any idea where she had come from. He was simply obsessed. His fingers were pulled towards her hair like needles to a magnet: he kept standing up and kissing her breasts, her shoulders, her ears. Bernard watched Raymond's fat tongue explore the coil of Melanie's ear with considerable distaste.

'Will you have coffee?' he said to Melanie in French. He indicated the coffee pot. She bent her head towards it with a quick curving movement, sniffed it, and then hovered briefly over the milk jug.

'This,' she said, indicating the hot milk. 'I will drink this.'

She looked at Bernard with huge black eyes under long lashes.

'I wish you joy,' said Bernard in Cévenol French, 'of your immortal soul.'

'Hey,' said Raymond, 'don't flirt with my girl in foreign languages.'

'I don't flirt,' said Bernard. 'I paint.'

'And we'll be off after breakfast and leave you to your painting,' said Raymond. 'Won't we, my sweet darling? Melanie wants – Melanie hasn't got – she didn't exactly bring – you understand – all her clothes and things. We're going to go to Cannes and buy some real clothes. Melanie wants to see the film festival and the stars. You won't mind, old friend, you didn't want me in the first place. I don't want to interrupt your *painting*. *Chacun à sa boue*, as we used to say in the army, I know that much French.'

Melanie held out her pretty fat hands and turned them over and over with considerable satisfaction. They were pinkly pale and also ornamented with pearly nail-varnish. She did not look at Raymond, simply twisted her head about with what could have been pleasure at his little sallies of physical attention, or could have been irritation. She did not speak. She smiled a little, over her milk, like a satisfied cat, displaying two rows of sweet little pearly teeth between her glossy pink lips.

Raymond's packing did not take long. Melanie turned out to have one piece of luggage – a large green leather bag full of rattling coins, by the sound. Raymond saw her into the car like a princess, and came back to say goodbye to his friend.

'Have a good time,' said Bernard. 'Beware of philosophers.'

'Where would I find any philosophers?' asked Raymond, who had done theatre design at art school with Bernard and now designed sets for a successful children's TV programme called *The A-Mazing Maze of Monsters*. 'Philosophers are extinct. I think your wits are turning, old friend, with stomping around on your own. You need a girlfriend.'

'I don't,' said Bernard. 'Have a good holiday.'

'We're going to be married,' said Raymond, looking surprised, as though he himself had not known this until he said it. The face of Melanie swam at the car window, the pearly teeth visible inside the soft lips, the dark eyes staring. 'I must go,' said Raymond. 'Melanie's waiting.'

Left to himself, Bernard settled back into the bliss of solitude. He looked at his latest work and saw that it was good. Encouraged, he looked at his earlier work and saw that that was good, too. All those blues, all those curious questions, all those almost-answers. The only problem was, where to go now. He walked up and down, he remembered the philosopher and laughed. He got out his Keats. He reread the dreadful moment in *Lamia* where the bride vanished away under the coldly malevolent eye of the sage.

> Do not all charms fly
> At the mere touch of cold philosophy?
> There was an awful rainbow once in heaven:
> We know her woof, her texture; she is given
> In the dull catalogue of common things.
> Philosophy will clip an Angel's wings,
> Conquer all mysteries by rule and line,
> Empty the haunted air and gnomed mine –
> Unweave a rainbow, as it erewhile made
> The tender-personed Lamia melt into a shade.

Personally, Bernard said to himself, he had never gone along with Keats about all that stuff. By philosophy Keats seems to mean natural science, and personally he, Bernard, would rather have the optical mysteries of waves and particles in the water and light of the rainbow than any old gnome or fay. He had been at least as interested in the problems of reflection and refraction when he had had the lovely snake in his pool as he had been in its oddity – in its *otherness* – as snakes went. He hoped that no natural scientist would come along and find Melanie's blood group to be that of some sort of herpes, or do an X-ray and see something odd in her spine. She made a very good blowzy sort of a woman, just right for Raymond. He wondered what sort of a woman she would have become for him, and dismissed the problem. He didn't want a woman. He wanted another visual idea. A mystery to be explained by rule and line. He looked around his breakfast table. A rather nondescript orange-brown butterfly was sipping the juice of the rejected peaches. It had a golden eye at the base of its wings and a rather lovely white streak, shaped like a tiny dragon-wing. It stood on the glistening rich yellow peach-flesh and manoeuvred its body to sip the sugary juices and suddenly it was not orange-brown at all, it was a rich, gleaming intense purple. And then it was both at once, orange-gold and purple-veiled, and then it was purple again, and then it folded its wings and the undersides had a purple eye and a soft green streak, and tan, and white edged with charcoal . . .

When he came back with his paintbox it was still turning and sipping. He mixed purple, he mixed orange, he made browns. It was done with a dusting of scales, with refractions of rays. The pigments were discovered and measured, the scales on the wings were noted and *seen*, everything was a mystery, serpents and water and light. He was off again. Exact study would not clip this creature's wings, it would dazzle his eyes with its brightness. Don't go, he begged it, watching and learning, don't go. Purple and orange is a terrible and violent fate. There is months of work in it. Bernard attacked it. He was happy, in one of the ways in which human beings are happy.

Cold

Façon de Venise goblet, 17th century

Cold

In a temperate kingdom, in the midst of a land-mass, with great meandering rivers but no seashores, with deciduous forests, and grassy plains, a princess was born on a blue summer day. She was eagerly awaited, although she was the thirteenth child, for the first twelve royal children were all princes, and her mother longed for gentle-ness and softness, whilst her powerful father longed for delicacy and beauty. She was born after a long labour, which lasted a day and a night, just as the sun began to colour the sky, but before it had warmed the earth. She was born, like most babies, squashed and livid, with a slicked cap of thick black hair. She was slight enough, but perfectly shaped, and when the nurses had washed off her protective waxy crust the blood began to run red and rapid, to the tips of her fine fingers and under the blue of her lips. She had a fine, transparent skin, so the blush of blood was fiery and rosy;

when her hair was washed, it sprang into a soft, black fur. She was pronounced – and was – beautiful. Her exhausted mother, whose own blood began to stir faster again as the child was laid on her breast, said she should be named 'Fiammarosa', a name that just came into her head at that moment, as a perfect description. Her father came in and picked her up in her new rosy shawl, holding the tiny creature clasped in his two huge hands, with her little red legs waving, and her composed pink face yawning perfectly above his thumbs. He was, like his father before him, like all the kings of that country, a large, strong, golden-bearded, deep-voiced, smiling man, a good soldier who avoided conflict, a good huntsman who never killed droves of creatures, but enjoyed the difficulty of the chase, the dark of the forests, the rush of the rivers. When he saw his daughter, he fell in love with her vulnerable fragility, as fathers do. No one shall ever hurt you, he said to the little creature, whose wavering hand brushed against the soft curls of his beard, whose fingers touched his warm lips. No one. He kissed his wife's damp brow, and she smiled.

When Fiammarosa was a few months old, the sooty first hair came out, as it does, in wisps and strands, collecting on her white lawn pillows. In its place, slowly and strongly, grew pale golden hair, so pale it shone silver when the light was in it, though it could be sunny-yellow seen against scalp, or brow, or, as it grew, on her narrow neck. As she drank in her mother's milk, she became milky; the flush faded as though it had never been, and the child's skin became softly pale, like white rose petals. Her bones were very fine, and the baby chubbiness all children assume before they move was only fleeting in her; she had sharp cheekbones, and a fine nose and chin, long, fine, sharp fingers and toes, even as an infant. Her eyes, under white brows and pearly eyelids, retained that dark, deep colour that is no colour, that in the newborn we call blue. The baby, said the nurse, was like fine bone china. She looked breakable. She behaved as though she herself thought she was fragile, moving little, and with a cautious carefulness. As she grew, and learned to crawl, and to walk, she grew thinner and whiter. The doctors pronounced her 'delicate'. She must be kept warm, they said, and rest frequently. She must be fed well, on nourishing things, things that would fill her out – she must drink concentrated soups, full of meat juices and rich with vegetables, she must have creams and zabagliones, fresh fruits and nourishing custards. This regime had a certain success. The white limbs filled out, the child's cheeks rounded over those edged bones, she acquired a pretty pout and faint dimples on her little fists. But with the milky flesh came languor. Her pale head dropped on its pale stalk. The gold hair lay flat and gleaming, unmoving like the surface of a still liquid. She walked at the right age, spoke at the right age, was docile and learned good manners without fuss. She had a habit of yawning, opening her shell-pink lips to show a row of perfect, gleaming, tiny white teeth, and a rosy tongue and gullet. She learned to put out a limp hand in front of this involuntary grimace, which had an aspect of intense laziness, and another aspect, her mother once thought, of a perfectly silent howl or cry.

Never was a young girl more loved. Her parents loved her, her nurses loved her, her twelve brothers, from the young men to the little boys, loved her, and tried to think of ways to please her, and to bring roses to the pale cheeks and a smile to the soft mouth. In spring weather, well-wrapped in lambswool shawls and fur bonnets, she was driven out in a little carriage, in which she lolled amongst soft cushions, staring indifferently at the trees and the sky. She had her own little rose-garden, with a pool full of rosy fish in green deeps, and a swing on which, in the warmest, brightest weather, her brothers pushed her gently to and fro, whilst she leaned her face on the cool chains and looked down at the grass. Picnics were brought out to this garden, and Fiammarosa reclined on a grassy slope, swathed in soft muslins, with a wide straw hat tied under her chin with pink ribbons, to protect her from sunburn. It was discovered that she had a taste for water-ices, flavoured with blackberry and raspberry, and for chilled slices of watermelon. These delicacies brought a fleeting smile to her normally expressionless face. She liked to lie on the grassy bank and watch her brothers play badminton, but any suggestion, as she grew older, that she might join in brought on an attack of yawning, a drooping, a retreat to the darkened rooms of the palace. Her brothers brought her presents; she was unimpressed by parakeets and kittens, but became curiously attached to a little silver hand-mirror, engraved with twining roses, from her eldest brother.

Her tutor loved her, too. He was a brilliant young man, destined to be a professor, who was writing a great history of the kingdom from its remotest beginnings, and had not wanted the court appointment at all. He loved her not despite, but because of, her lethargy. He was sorry for her. There were days when, for no reason he could discern, she was able to sit upright and concentrate, infrequent days when she suddenly surprised him with a page of elegant calculations, or an opinion as piercingly clever as it was unexpected, on a poem or a drawing he was discussing with her. She was no fool, Fiammarosa, but there was no life in her, most of the time. She yawned. She drooped. He would leave their study to fetch a book, and return to find the white head dropped on to the circle of the milky arms on the table, a picture of lassitude and boredom, or, just possibly, of despair. He asked her, on one of these days, if she felt ill, and she said, no, why should she?, directing at him a blank, gentle, questioning look. I feel much as usual, she said. Much as I always feel. She spoke, he thought, with a desperate patience. He closed the window, to keep out the draught.

During her early years, the earth went through one of its periodic coolings. Autumn came earlier and earlier, the rose leaves were blown about the enclosed garden, there was a nip in the air in late summer, and snow on the ground before the turn of the year. The palace people redoubled their efforts to protect the princess, installing velvet curtains and bed-hangings. On very cold nights, they lit a fire in the pretty fireplace in her bedroom, so that the coloured streamers of reflected flames chased each other across the carved ceiling, and moved in the soft hangings on the walls. Fiammarosa was now at the edge of girlhood, almost a woman, and her dreams troubled her. She dreamed of dark blue spaces, in which she travelled, without moving a muscle, at high speeds above black and white fields and forests. In her dreams she heard the wind coil, howling, round the outside walls, and its shriek woke her, so that she heard with her ears what she had dreamed in her skull. The wind spoke with many voices, soft and shrill, rushing and eddying. Fiammarosa wanted to see it. She felt stifled in her soft blankets, in her lambswool gown. She went to the window, and dragged open the curtain. Behind it, her breath, the breath of the room, had frozen into white and glistening feathers and flowers on the glass, into illusory, disproportionate rivers with tributaries and frozen falls. Through these transparent, watery forms she could see the lawns and bushes, under snow, and the long tips of icicles poured down from the eaves above her. She put her cheek against the frozen tracery, and felt a bite, a burn, that was both painful and intensely pleasurable. Her soft skin adhered, ever so slightly, to the ice. Her eyes took in the rounded forms of the lawns under snow, the dark blue shadows across it, the glitter where the light from her window sliced it, and the paler glitter where the moonlight touched the surface. And her body came alive with the desire to lie out there, on that whiteness, face-to-face with it, fingertips and toes pushing into the soft crystals. The whole of her short, cosseted history was against her; she drew back from the glass, telling herself that although the snow blanket looked soft and pretty it was dangerous and threatening; its attraction was an illusion of the glass.

But all the next day, she was possessed by this image of her own naked body, stretched on a couch of snow. And the next night, when the palace was dark and silent, she put on a flowered silk wrap, covered with summer poppies, and crept down the stairs, to see if there was a way out into the garden. But all the doors she could find were locked and barred, and she was discovered by a patrolling guardsman, to whom she said, with a tentative smile, that she had come down because she was hungry. He was not to know that she always had sweet biscuits by her bed. So he took her to the kitchen, and poured a glass of milk for her in the larder, and found her some white bread and jam, which she nibbled, still smiling at him, as she questioned him about his work, the places where the keys were kept, the times of his patrols.

When she followed him into the larder, as he ladled milk from a great stone jar in the light of a candle, she felt cold rise from the stone floor, and pour from the thick walls, and sing outside the open grated window. The guard begged her to go into the kitchen – 'You will catch your death in this draught,' he said – but the Princess was stretching her fingers to touch the eddying air.

She thanked him prettily, and went back to her hot little room where, after a moment's thought, she took her wrought-iron poker and broke up the banked coals of her fire, feeling faint as she hung over it, with the smoke and the bright sparks, but happy, as the life went out of the coals, the reds burned darker, and were replaced by fine white ash, like the snow. Then she took off her gown, and rolled open the nest of bedclothes, and pulled back the great curtains – it was not possible to open the window – and lay back, feeling the sweat of her efforts cool delectably in the crevices of her skin.

The next night she reconnoitred the corridors and cupboards, and the night after that she went down in the small hours, and took a small key from a hook, a key that unlocked a minor side-door that led to the kitchen-garden, which was now, like everywhere else, under deep snow, the taller herbs stiffly draggled, the tufted ones humped under white, the black branches brittle with the white coating frozen along their upper edges. It was full moon. Everything was black and white and silver. The princess crept in her slippers between the beds of herbs, and then bent down impulsively and pulled off the slippers. The cold snow on the soles of her feet gave her the sense of bliss that most humans associate with warm frills of water at the edge of summer seas, with sifted sand, with sunny stone. She ran faster. Her blood hummed. Her pale hair floated in the wind of her own movement in the still night. She went under an arch and out through a long ride, running lightly under dark, white-encrusted boughs, into what in summer was a meadow. She did not know why she did what she did next. She had always been decorous and docile. Her body was full of an electric charge, a thrill, from an intense cold. She threw off her silk wrap, and her creamy woollen nightgown, and lay for a moment, as she had imagined lying, with her naked skin on the cold white sheet. She did not sink; the crust was icy and solid. All along her body, in her knees, her thighs, her small round belly, her pointed breasts, the soft inner skin of her arms, she felt an intense version of that paradoxical burn she had received from the touch of the frosted window. The snow did not numb Fiammarosa; it pricked and hummed and brought her, intensely, to life. When her front was quite chilled, she turned over on her back, and lay there, safe inside the form of her own faint impression on the untouched surface. She stared up, at the great moon with its slaty shadows on its white-gold disc, and the huge fields of scattered, clustered, far-flung glittering wheeling stars in the deep darkness, white on midnight, and she was, for the first time in her life, happy. This is who I am, the cold princess thought to herself, wriggling for sheer pleasure in the snow-dust, this is what I want. And when she was quite cold, and completely alive and crackling with energy, she rose to her feet, and began a strange, leaping dance, pointing sharp fingers at the moon, tossing her long mane of silver hair, sparkling with ice-crystals, circling and bending and finally turning cartwheels under the wheeling sky. She could feel the cold penetrating her surfaces, all over, insistent and relentless. She even thought that some people might have thought that this was painful. But for her, it was bliss. She went in with the dawn, and lived through the day in an alert, suspended, dreaming state, waiting for the deep dark, and another excursion into the cold.

Night after night, now, she went and danced in the snowfield. The deep frost held and she began to be able to carry some of her cold energy back into her daily work. At the same time, she began to notice changes in her body. She was growing thinner, rapidly – the milky softness induced by her early regime was replaced with a slender, sharp, bony beauty. And one night, as she moved, she found that her whole body was encased in a transparent, crackling skin of ice that broke into spiderweb-fine veined sheets as she danced and then re-formed. The sensation of this double skin was delicious. She had frozen eyelashes and saw the world through an ice-lens; her tossing hair made a brittle and musical sound, for each hair was coated and frozen. The faint sounds of shivering and splintering and clashing made a kind of whispered music as she danced on. In the daytime now, she could barely keep awake, and her night-time skin persisted patchily in odd places, at the nape of her neck, around her wrists, like bracelets. She tried to sit by the window, in her lessons, and also tried surreptitiously to open it, to let in the cold wind, when Hugh, her tutor, was briefly out of the room. And then, one day, she came down, rubbing frost out of her eyelashes with rustling knuckles, and found the window wide open, Hugh wrapped in a furred jacket, and a great book open on the table.

'Today,' said Hugh, 'we are going to read the history of your ancestor, King Beriman, who made an expedition to the kingdoms beyond the mountains, in the frozen North, and came back with an icewoman.'

Fiammarosa considered Hugh.

'Why?' she said, putting her white head on one side, and looking at him with sharp, pale blue eyes between the stiff lashes.

'I'll show you,' said Hugh, taking her to the

open window. 'Look at the snow on the lawns, in the rose-garden.'

And there, lightly imprinted, preserved by the frost, were the tracks of fine bare feet, running lightly, skipping, eddying, dancing.

Fiammarosa did not blush; her whiteness became whiter, the ice-skin thicker. She was alive in the cold air of the window.

'Have you been watching me?'

'Only from the window,' said Hugh, 'to see that you came to no harm. You can see that the only footprints are fine, and elegant, and naked. If I had followed you I should have left tracks.'

'I see,' said Fiammarosa.

'And,' said Hugh, 'I have been watching you since you were a little girl, and I recognise happiness and health when I see it.'

'Tell me about the icewoman.'

'Her name was Fror. She was given by her father, as a pledge for a truce between the ice-people and King Beriman. The chronicles describe her as wondrously fair and slender, and they say also that King Beriman loved her distractedly, and that she did not return his love. They say she showed an ill will, liked to haunt caverns and rivers and refused to learn the language of this kingdom. They say she danced by moonlight, on the longest night, and that there were those in the kingdom who believed she was a witch, who had enchanted the King. She was seen, dancing naked, with three white hares, which were thought to be creatures of witchcraft, under the moon, and she was imprisoned in the cells under the palace. There she gave birth to a son, who was taken from her, and given to his father. And the priests wanted to burn the icewoman, "to melt her stubbornness and punish her stiffness", but the King would not allow it.

'Then one day, three northmen came riding to the gate of the castle, tall men with axes on white horses, and said they had come "to take back our woman to her own air". No one knew how they had been summoned: the priests said that it was by witchcraft that she had called to them from her stone cell. It may have been. It seems clear that there was a threat of war if the woman was not relinquished. So she was fetched out, and "wrapped in a cloak to cover her thinness and decay" and told she could ride away with her kinsmen. The chronicler says she did not ask to see her husband or her tiny son, but "cold and unfeeling as she had come" mounted behind one of the northmen and they turned and rode away together.

'And King Beriman died not long after, of a broken heart or of witchcraft, and his brother reigned until Leonin was old enough to be crowned. The chronicler says that Leonin made a "warm-blooded and warm-hearted" ruler, as though the blood of his forefathers ran true in him, and the "frozen lymph" of his maternal stock was melted away to nothing.

'But I believe that after generations, a lost face, a lost being, can find a form again.'

'You think I am an icewoman.'

'I think you carry the inheritance of that northern princess. I think also that her nature was much misunderstood, and that what appeared to be kindness was extreme cruelty – paradoxically, probably her life was preserved by what appeared to be the cruellest act of those who held her here, the imprisonment in cold stone walls, the thin prison dress, the bare diet.'

'I felt that in my bones, listening to your story.'

'It is *your* story, Princess. And you too are framed for cold. You must live – when the thaw comes – in cool places. There are ice-houses in the palace gardens – we must build more, and stock them with blocks of ice, before the snow melts.'

Fiammarosa smiled at Hugh with her sharp mouth. She said:

'You have read my desires. All through my childhood I was barely alive. I felt constantly that I must collapse, vanish, fall into a faint, stifle. Out there, in the cold, I am a living being.'

'I know.'

'You choose your words very tactfully, Hugh. You told me I was "framed for cold". That is a statement of natural philosophy, and time. It may be that I have ice in my veins, like the icewoman, or something that boils and steams at normal temperatures, and flows busily in deep frost. But you did not tell me I had a cold nature. The icewoman did not look back at her husband and son. Perhaps she was cold in her soul, as well as in her veins?'

'That is for you to say. It is so long ago, the tale of the icewoman. Maybe she saw King Beriman only as a captor and conqueror? Maybe she loved someone else, in the North, in the snow? Maybe she felt as you feel, on a summer's day, barely there, yawning for faintness, moving in shadows.'

'How do you know how I feel, Hugh?'

'I watch you. I study you. I love you.'

Fiammarosa noticed, in her cool mind, that she did not love Hugh, whatever love was.

She wondered whether this was a loss, or a gain. She was inclined to think, on balance, that it was a gain. She had been so much loved, as a little child, and all that heaping of anxious love had simply made her feel ill and exhausted. There was more life in coldness. In solitude. Inside a crackling skin of protective ice that was also a sensuous delight.

After this clarification, even when the thaw came, and the snow ran away, and fell in damp, crashing masses from the roof and the branches, Fiammarosa's life was better. Hugh convinced the King and Queen that their daughter needed to be cold to survive, and the ingenuity that had been put into keeping her warm and muffled was diverted, on his suggestion, into the construction of ice-houses, and cool bedrooms with stone walls on the north side of the palace. The new Fiammarosa was full of spiky life. She made little gardens of mountain snow-plants around her ice-retreats, which stood like so many summer-houses in the woods and the gardens. No one accused her of witchcraft – this was a later age – but there was perhaps a little less love for this coldly shining, fiercely energetic, sharp being than there had been for the milky girl in her rosy cushions. She studied snow-crystals and ice formations under a magnifying glass, in the winter, and studied the forms of her wintry flowers and mosses in the summer. She became an artist – all princesses are compelled to be artists, they must spin, or draw, or embroider, and she had always dutifully done so, producing heaps of cushions and walls of good-enough drawings. She hated 'good enough' but had had to be content with it. Now she began to weave tapestries, with silver threads and ice-blue threads, with night violets and cool primroses, which mixed the geometric forms of the snow-crystals with the delicate forms of the moss and rosettes of petals, and produced shimmering, intricate tapestries that were much more than 'good enough', that were unlike anything seen before in that land. She became an assiduous correspondent, writing to gardeners and natural philosophers, to spinners of threads and weavers all over the world. She was happy, and in the winter, when the world froze again under an iron-grey sky, she was ecstatic.

Princesses, also, are expected to marry. They are expected to marry for dynastic reasons, to cement an alliance, to placate a powerful rival, to bear royal heirs. They are, in the old stories, gifts and rewards, handed over by their loving fathers to heroes and adventurers who must undergo trials, or save people. It would appear, Fiammarosa had thought as a young girl, reading both histories and wonder tales, that princesses are commodities. But also, in the same histories and tales, it can be seen that this is not so. Princesses are captious and clever choosers. They tempt and test their suitors, they sit like spiders inside walls adorned with the skulls of the unsuccessful, they require super-human feats of strength and cunning from their suitors, and are not above helping out, or weeping over, those who appeal to their hearts. They follow their chosen lovers through rough deserts, and ocean tempests, they ride on the wings of the north wind and enlist the help of ants and eagles, trout and mice, hares and ducks, to rescue these suddenly helpless husbands from the clutches of scheming witches, or ogre-kings. They do have, in real life, the power to reject and some power to choose. They are wooed. She had considered her own cold heart in this context and had thought that she would do better, ideally, to remain unmarried. She was too happy alone to make a good bride. She could not think out a course of action entirely but had vaguely decided upon a course of prevarication and intimidation, if suitors presented themselves. For their own sakes, as much as for her own. She was sorry, in the abstract – she thought a great deal in the abstract, it suited her – for anyone who should love her, or think it a good idea to love her. She did not believe she was truly lovable. Beside her parents, and her brothers, whose love was automatic and unseeing, the only person who truly loved her was Hugh. And her cold eye, and her cold mind, had measured the gulf between what Hugh felt for her and what she felt for him.

She tried never to let it show; she was grateful, his company was comfortable to her. But both he and she were intelligent beings, and both knew how things stood.

The King had his own ideas, which he believed were wise and subtle, about all this. He believed his daughter needed to marry more than most women. He believed she needed to be softened and opened to the world, that she had inherited from the unsatisfactory icewoman a dangerous, brittle edge which would hurt her more than anyone else. He believed it would be good for his daughter to be melted smooth, though he did not, in his thinking, push this metaphor too far. He had a mental image of an icicle running with water, not of an absent icicle and a warm, formless pool. He thought the sensible thing would be to marry this cold creature to a prince from the icelands from which the original Fror had been snatched by King Beriman, and he sent letters to Prince Boris, beyond the mountains, with a sample of his daughter's weaving, and a painting of her white beauty, her fine bones, blue eyes and cool gold hair. He was a great believer in protocol, and protocol had always, at these times, meant that the picture and the invitation must go to many princes, and not only one. There must be a feast, and something of a competition. What happened customarily was that the Princess's portrait would go simultaneously (allowing for the vagaries of horses and camels, galleons and mule trains) to many eligible princes. The princes, in turn, on receiving the portrait, would return gifts, sumptuous gifts, striking gifts, to the king, to be given to the Princess. And if she found them acceptable (or if her father did), then the princes would make the journey in person, and the Princess, in person, would make her choice. In this way, the King offended none of his proud neighbours, leaving the choice to the whim, or the aesthetic inclination, of the young woman herself. Of course, if there were any pressing reason why one alliance was more desirable than another, most fathers would enlighten their daughters, and some would exhort or threaten. In the case of Fiammarosa none of this applied. Her father wished her to marry for her own good, and he wished her to marry Prince Boris simply because his kingdom was cold and full of icebergs and glaciers, where she would be at home. But he did not say this, for he knew that women are perverse.

The portraits, the letters, dispersed through the known world. After a time, the presents began to return. A small golden envoy from the East brought a silken robe, flame-coloured, embroidered with peacocks, light as air. A rope of pearls, black, rose, and luminous pale ones, the size of larks' eggs, came from an island kingdom, and a three-dimensional carved chess game, all in different jades, with little staircases and turrets edged with gold, came from a tiny country between two deserts. There were heaps of gold and silver plates, a leopard in a cage, which sickened and died, a harp, a miniature pony, and an illuminated treatise on necromancy. The King and Queen watched Fiammarosa as she gravely thanked the messengers. She appeared to be interested in the mechanism of an Orcalian musical box, but only *scientifically* interested, so to speak. Then Prince Boris's envoy arrived, a tall fair man with a gold beard and two gold plaits, riding a hairy, flea-bitten warhorse, and followed by packhorses with great pine chests. He opened these with a flourish, and brought out a robe of silver fox-fur, an extra-ordinary bonnet, hung with the black-tipped tails of ermine stoats, and a whalebone box, polished like a new tooth, containing a necklace of bears' claws threaded on a silver chain. The Princess put her thin hands, involuntarily, to her slender throat. The envoy said that the necklace had been worn by Prince Boris's mother, and by her mother before her. He was clad in fleeces and wore a huge circu-lar fur hat coming down over his ears. Fiammarosa said that the gifts were magnificent. She said this so gracefully that her mother looked to see if some ancestral inkling in her responded to bears' claws. There was no colour at all in her lips, or in her cheeks, but with her that could be a sign of pleasure – she whitened, where other women blushed. The King thought to himself that a man and his gifts were not the same thing. He thought that the narrow neck would have a barbaric beauty, circled by the polished sharp claws, but he did not wish to see it.

The last envoy declared that he was not the last envoy, having been parted from his fellows on their dangerous voyage. They had travelled separately, so that one at least of them might arrive with his gift. Prince Sasan, he said, had been much moved by the Princess's portrait. She was the woman he had seen in his dreams, said the envoy, lyrically. The Princess, whose dreams entertained no visitors, only white spaces, wheeling birds and snowflakes, smiled composedly, without warmth. The envoy's gift took a long time to unwrap. It was packed in straw, and fine leather, and silk. When it was revealed, it appeared at first sight to be a rough block of ice. Then, slowly, it was seen to be a glass palace, within the ice, so to speak, as hallucinatory turrets and chambers, fantastic carvings and pillars, reveal themselves in the ice and snow of mountain peaks. But once the eye had learned to read the irregularities of the surface, the magnifications and the tunnels within the block, it was seen to be a most cunningly wrought and regularly shaped transparent castle, within whose shining walls corridors ran into fretted chambers, staircases (with carved balustrades) mounted and descended in spirals and curves, in which thrones and pompous curtained beds stood in glistening cubicles, in which miraculous fine curtains of translucent glass floated between archways in still space. The glass castle was large enough for the centre to be hidden from the eye, though all the wide landings, the narrow passages, the doors and gangways, directed the eye to where the thickness of the transparent glass itself resisted penetration. Fiammarosa touched its cool surface with a cool finger. She was entranced by the skill of the layering. It was all done in a crystal-clear glass, with a green-blue tinge to it in places, and a different green-blue conferred simply by thickness itself. The eye looked through, and through, and in. Light went through, and through, and in. Solid walls of light glittered and, seen through their substance, trapped light hung in bright rooms like bubbles. There was one other colour, in all the perspectives of blue, green, and clear. From the dense, invisible centre little tongues of rosy flame (made of glass) ran along the corridors, mounted, gleaming, in the stairwells and hall-ways, threaded like ribbons round galleries, separated, and joined again as flames do, round pillars and gates. Behind a curtain of blue, a thread of rose and flame shone and twisted. The Princess walked round, and back, looking in. 'It is an image of my master's heart,' said the lyrical envoy. 'It is a poetic image of his empty life, which awaits the delicate warmth of the Princess Fiammarosa in every chamber. He has been set on fire by his vision of the portrait of the Princess.'

The envoy was a sallow young man, with liquid brown eyes. The bluff King and the careful Queen were not impressed by his rhetoric. The Princess went on walking round the glass block, staring in. It was not clear that she had heard his latest remarks.

The second envoy from Prince Sasan arrived a few days later, dusty and travel-worn, another sallow man with brown eyes. His gift was dome-shaped. He too, as he unwrapped it, spoke lyrically of the contents. He did not appear to be speaking to a script; lyricism appeared to spring naturally to the lips of the Sasanians. His gift, he said, was an image, a metaphor, a symbol, for the sweetness and light, the summer world which the thought of the Princess had created in the mind of his master.

The second gift was also made of glass. It was a beehive, a transparent, shining form constructed of layers of hexagonal cells, full of white glass grubs, and amber-coloured glass honey. Over the surface of the cells crawled, and in the solid atmosphere hung and floated, wonderfully wrought insects, with furry bodies, veined wings, huge eyes and fine antennae. They even carried bags of golden pollen on their black, thread-glass legs. Around the hive were glass flowers with petals of crumpled and gleaming yellow glass, with crowns of fine stamens, with blue bells and fine-throated purple hoods. A fat bee was half-buried in the heart of a spotted snapdragon. Another uncoiled a proboscis and sipped the heart of a campanula. So, said the lyrical envoy, was the heart of his master touched by the warm thought of the Princess, so was love seeded, and sweetness garnered, in the garden of his heart. Hugh thought that this might be too much for his austere pupil, but she was not listening. She had laid her cool cheek against the cool glass dome, as if to catch the soundless hum of the immobile spun-glass wings.

The third envoy arrived bloodied and incoherent. He had been set upon by bandits and had been forced to hide his package in a hollow tree, from which he had retrieved it, late at night. He unpacked it before the court, murmuring incoherently, 'So delicate, I shall be tortured, never forgiven, has harm come to it?' His package was in two parts, tall and cylindrical, fat and spherical. Out of the cylindrical part came a tall glass stem, and a series of fine, fine, glass rods, olive-green, amber, white, which he built, breathing heavily, into an extraordinarily complex web of branches and twigs. It was large – the height, maybe, of a two-year-old child. Folded into his inner garments he had a plan of the intervals of the sprouting of the branches. The assembly took a long time – the Queen suggested that they go and take refreshment and leave the poor, anxious man to complete his labour unobserved and in peace, but Fiammarosa was entranced. She watched each slender stem find its place, breathing quietly, staring intently. The spherical parcel proved to contain a pleroma of small spherical parcels, all nestling together, from which the envoy took a whole world of flowers, fruit, twining creepers, little birds, frost-forms and ice-forms. Part of the tree he hung with buds, tight and bursting, mossy and glistening, rosy and sooty-black. Then he hung blossoms of every kind, apple and cherry, magnolia and catkins, hypericum and chestnut candles. Then he added, radiating among all these, the fruits, oranges and lemons, silver pears and golden apples, rich plums and damsons, ruddy pomegranates and clustered translucent crimson berries and grapes with the bloom on them. Each tiny element was in itself an example of virtuoso glass-making. When he had hung the flowers and the fruit, he perched the birds, a red cardinal, a white dove, a black-capped rosy-breasted bullfinch, a blue Australian wren, an iridescent kingfisher, a blackbird with a gold beak, and in the centre, on the crest of the branches, a bird of paradise with golden eyes in its midnight tail, and a crest of flame. Then he hung winter on the remaining branches, decorating sharp black twigs with filigree leaf skeletons, flounces of snow, and sharp icicles, catching the light and making rainbows in the air. This, he said breathlessly, was his master's world as it would be if the Princess consented to be his wife, a paradise state with all seasons in one, and the tree of life flowering and fruiting perpetually. There is bleak winter, too, said the Princess, setting an icicle in motion. The envoy looked soulfully at her and said that the essential sap of trees lived through the frost, and so it was with the tree of life, of which this was only an image.

The Princess did not leave the tree for the rest of the day. Look, she said to Hugh, at the rich patterning of the colours, look at the way the light shines in the globes of the fruit, the seeds of the pomegranate, the petals of the flowers. Look at the beetles in the clefts of the trunk, like tiny jewels, look at the feathers in the spun-glass tail of the bird. What kind of a man would have made this?

'Not a prince, a craftsman,' said Hugh, a little jealous. 'A prince merely finds the best man, and pays him. A prince, at most, makes the metaphor, and the craftsman carries it out.'

'I make my own weaving,' said the Princess. 'I design and I weave my own work. It is possible that a prince made the castle, the hive and the tree.'

'It is possible,' said Hugh. 'A prince with a taste for extravagant metaphor.'

'Would you prefer a necklace of bears' claws,' asked the icewoman, 'if you were a woman? Would you?'

'A man and his gifts are two things,' said Hugh. 'And glass is not ice.'

'What do you mean?' asked the Princess. But Hugh would say no more.

The princes arrived, after a month or two, in person. Five had made the journey, Prince Boris, the plump dusky prince who had sent the pearls, the precise, silk-robed prince who had sent the silk robe, the curly, booted and spurred prince who had sent the chess game, and Prince Sasan, who arrived last, having travelled furthest. Prince Boris, the King thought, was a fine figure of a man, strong like an oak-tree, with golden plaits and a golden beard. His pale-blue eyes were icy pools, but there were wrinkles of laughter in their corners. Prince Sasan rode up on a fine-boned, delicate horse, black as soot, and trembling with nerves. He insisted on seeing to its stabling himself, though he was accompanied by a meagre retinue of squires with the same sallow skins and huge brown eyes as the envoys. His own hair was black, like his horse, and hung, fine and dry and very straight, in a dark fringe, and a dark curtain, ending at his shoulders. He was a small man, a little shorter than Fiammarosa, but his shoulders were powerful. His face was narrow and his skin dark gold. His nose was sharp and arched, his brows black lines, his lashes long and dark over dark eyes, deeper-set than the envoys'. Prince Boris had a healthy laugh, but Prince Sasan was cat-like and silent. He made his bows, and spoke his greetings, and then appeared content to watch events as though he were the audience, not the actor. He took Fiammarosa's hand in his thin hand, when he met her, and lifted it to his lips, which were thin and dry. 'Enchanted,' said Prince Sasan. 'Delighted,' said the icewoman, coolly. That was all.

The visits were the occasion of much diplomacy and various energetic rides and hunting expeditions, on which, since it was high summer, the Princess did not join the company. In the evenings, there were feasts, and musical entertainments. The island prince had brought two porcelain-skinned ladies who played exquisite tinkling tunes on xylophones. The curly prince had a minstrel with a harp, and Prince Boris had two huntsmen who played a rousing, and blood-curdling, duet on hunting-horns. The Princess was sitting between Boris and the curly prince, and had been hearing tales of the long winters, the Northern Lights, the floating icebergs. Prince Sasan beckoned his squire, who unwrapped a long black pipe, with a reed mouthpiece, from a scarlet silk cloth. This he handed to the Prince, who set it to his own lips, and blew one or two tentative notes, reedy, plangent, to set the pitch. 'I based this music,' he said, looking down at the table, 'on the songs of the goat-herds.' He began to play. It was music unlike anything they had ever heard. Long, long, wavering breaths, with pure notes chasing each other through them; long calls which rose and rose, trembled and danced on the air, fell, whis-pered, and vanished. Circlings of answering phrases, flights, bird-cries, rest. The Princess's mind was full of water frozen in mid-fall, or find-ing a narrow channel between ribs and arches of ice. When the strange piping came to an end, everyone complimented the Prince on his playing.

Hugh said, 'I have never heard such long phrases ride on one breath.'

'I have good lungs,' said Prince Sasan. 'Glass-blower's lungs.'

'The glass is your own work?' said the Princess.

'Of course it is,' said Prince Sasan.

The Princess said that it was very beautiful. Prince Sasan said:

'My country is not rich, though it is full of space, and I think it is beautiful. I cannot give you precious stones. My country is largely desert: we have an abundance only of sand, and glass-blowing is one of our ancient crafts. All Sasanian princes are glass-blowers. The secrets are handed on from generation to generation.'

'I did not know glass was made from sand,' said the Princess. 'It resembles frozen water.'

'It is sand, melted and fused,' said Prince Sasan. His eyes were cast down.

'In a furnace of flames,' said Hugh, impulsively. 'It is melted and fused in a furnace of flames.'

The Princess trembled slightly. Prince Sasan lifted his gaze, and his black look met her blue one. There were candles between them, and she saw golden flames reflected in his dark eyes, whilst he saw white flames in her clear ones. She knew she should look away, and did not. Prince Sasan said:

'I have come to ask you to be my wife, and to come with me to my land of sand-dunes and green sea-waves and shores. Now I have seen you, I – '

He did not finish the sentence.

Prince Boris said that deserts were monotonous and hot. He said he was sure the Princess would prefer mountains and forests and rushing cold winds.

The Princess trembled a little more. Prince Sasan made a deprecating gesture with his thin hand, and stared into his plate, which contained sliced peaches, in red wine, on a nest of crushed ice.

'I will come with you to the desert,' said the Princess. 'I will come with you to the desert, and learn about glass-blowing.'

'I am glad of that,' said Prince Sasan. 'For I do not know how I should have gone on, if you had not.'

And amidst the mild uproar caused by the departure from protocol, and the very real panic and fear of the King and Queen and Hugh, the two of them sat and looked steadily across the table at the reflected flames in each other's eyes.

Once it became clear that the Princess's mind was made up, those who loved her stopped arguing, and the wedding took place. Fiammarosa asked Hugh to come with her to her new home, and he answered that he could not. He could not live in a hot climate, he told her, with his very first note of sharpness. Fiammarosa was glittering, restless and brittle with love. Hugh saw that she could not see him, that she saw only the absent Sasan, that dark, secret face imposed on his own open one. And he did not know, he added, having set his course, how she herself would survive. Love changes people, Fiammarosa told him in a small voice. Human beings are adaptable, said the icewoman. If I use my intelligence, and my willpower, she said, I shall be able to live there; I shall certainly die if I cannot be with the man on whom my heart is set. He will melt you into a puddle, Hugh told her, but only silently, and in his mind. She had never been so beautiful as she was in her wedding gown, white as snow, with lace like frost-crystals, with a sash blue as thick ice, and her pale face sharp with happiness and desire in the folds of transparent veiling.

The young pair spent the first week of their marriage in her old home, before setting out on the long journey to her new one. All eyes were on them, each day, as they came down from their bed-chamber to join the company. The housemaids whispered of happily bloodstained sheets – much rumpled, they added, most vigorously disturbed. The Queen observed to the King that the lovers had eyes only for each other, and he observed, a little sorrowfully, that this was indeed so. His daughter's sharp face grew sharper, and her eyes grew bluer and clearer; she could be seen to sense the presence of the dark Sasan behind her head, across a room, through a door. He moved quietly, like a cat, the southern prince, speaking little, and touching no one, except his wife. He could hardly prevent himself from touching her body, all over, in front of everyone, Hugh commented to himself, watching the flicker of the fine fingers down her back as the Prince bent to bestow an unnecessary kiss of greeting after a half-hour absence. Hugh noticed also that there were faint rosy marks on the Princess's skin, as though it had been scored, or lashed. Flushed lines in the hollow of her neck, inside her forearm where the sleeve fell away. He wanted to ask if she was hurt, and once opened his mouth to do so, and closed it again when he saw that she was not listening to him, that she was staring over his shoulder at a door where a moment later Sasan himself was to appear. If she was hurt, Hugh knew, because he knew her, she was also happy.

Fiammarosa's honeymoon nights were indeed a fantastic mixture of pleasure and pain. She and her husband, in a social way, were intensely shy with each other. They said little, and what they said was of the most conventional kind: Fiammarosa at least heard her own clear voice, from miles away, like that of a polite stranger sharing the room in which their two silent selves simmered with passion. And Sasan, whose dark eyes never left hers when they were silent, looked down at the sheets or out of the window when he spoke, and she knew in her heart that his unfinished, whispered sentences sounded as odd to him as her silver platitudes did to her. But when he touched her, his warm, dry fingers spoke to her skin, and when she touched his nakedness she was laughing and crying at once with delight over his golden warmth, his secret softness, the hard, fine arch of his bones. An icewoman's sensations are different from those of other women, but Fiammarosa could not know how different, for she had no standards of comparison; she could not name the agonising bliss that took possession of her. Ice burns, and it is hard to the warm-skinned to distinguish one sensation, fire, from the other, frost. Touching Sasan's heat was like and unlike the thrill of ice. Ordinary women melt, or believe themselves to be melting, to be running away like avalanches or rivers at the height of passion, and this, too, Fiammarosa experienced with a difference, as though her whole being were becoming liquid except for some central icicle, which was running with waterdrops that threatened to melt that too, to nothing. And at the height of her bliss she desired to take the last step, to nothing, to nowhere, and the next moment cried out in fear of annihilation. The fine brown fingers prised open the pale-blue eyelids. 'Are you there?'

asked the soft whisper. 'Where are you?' and she sighed, and returned.

When the morning light came into the room it found them curled together in a nest of red and white sheets. It revealed also marks, all over the pale cool skin: handprints round the narrow waist, sliding impressions from delicate strokes, like weals, raised rosy discs where his lips had rested lightly. He cried out, when he saw her, that he had hurt her. No, she said, she was part icewoman, it was her nature, she had an icewoman's skin that responded to every touch by blossoming red. Sasan still stared, and repeated, I have hurt you. No, no, said Fiammarosa, they are the marks of pleasure, pure pleasure. I shall cover them up, for only we ourselves should see our happiness.

But inside her a little melted pool of water slopped and swayed where she had been solid and shining.

The journey to the new country was long and arduous. Fiammarosa wrapped herself in a white hooded cloak, to reflect the sunlight away from her, and wore less and less inside it, as they rode south, through dark forests, and out on to grassy plains. They embarked, in a port where neither of them spoke the language, in the Sasanian boat that had been waiting for them, and sailed for weeks across the sea, in breezy weather, in a sudden storm, through two days and nights of glassy calm. Sasan enjoyed the voyage. He had a bucket with a glass bottom which he would let down into the green water to watch the creatures that floated and swam in the depth. He wore no more than a wrap round his narrow hips, and during the calm, he went overboard and swam around and under the boat, calling out to Fiammarosa, who sat swathed in white, wilting a little, on the deck, and answered breathlessly. He would bring glasses and buckets of the sea water on deck, and study the bubbles and ripples. He liked also to look at the sleek sea-surface in the moonlight, the gloss on the little swellings and subsidings, the tracks of phosphorescence. Fiammarosa was happier in the moonlight. It was cooler. She sat in a thin gown in the night air and smiled as her husband displayed his drawings and discoveries of translucency and reflection. He played his strange flute, and she listened, rapt. They sailed on. Every day was a little warmer. Every day the air was a little thicker, a little hotter.

When they came to the major port of Sasania, which was also its capital city, they were welcomed into the harbour by a flotilla of small boats bearing drummers and flautists, singers and cymbal-clashers. Fiammarosa nearly fell when her foot touched land; the stone of the harbour-steps was burning to the touch, and the sun was huge and glaring in a cobalt-blue sky with no clouds and no movement of air. She made a joke about the earth moving, after the movement of the waves, but the thought she had was that her temperate summers, with their bright flowers and birdsong, had no con-nection to this hot blue arch in which a few kites wheeled, slowly. The people had prepared a cur-tained litter for their delicate new queen, and so she was able to subside, panting, on to cushions, wondering if she would survive.

The palace was white and glistening, as though it was moulded from sugar. It had domes and towers, plain and blind and geometrically simple and beautiful. It was designed to keep out the sun, and inside it was a geometric maze of cool corridors, tiled in coloured glass, lit only by narrow slits of windows, which were glazed in beautiful colours, garnet, emerald, sapphire, which cast bright flames of coloured light on the floors. It was a little like a beehive, and inside its central dome a woven lattice-work of coloured light was spun by tiny loopholes and slits in the surface, shifting and changing as the sun moved in the dark bright sky outside. Optimism returned to Fiammarosa when she saw these dark corridors, these dim spaces. Icewomen like bright light, bright cold light, off-white; and darkness and confinement oppress them. But the molten heat outside oppressed her more. And there was so much in the palace to delight her senses. There was fruit on glass dishes, pearly and iridescent, smoky amber, translucent rose and indigo. There were meditative flute-players dropping strings of sound all day into the still air from little stools under the loopholes on the turns of the stairs. There were wonderful white jugs of latticino work, with frivolous frilled lips, containing pomegranate juices or lemonade, or swaying dark wine. Her own apartment had a circular window of stained glass, a white rose, fold on fold, on a peacock-blue ground. Within the heavy doors hung curtains of tiny glass beads of every conceivable colour, shimmering and twinkling. Round the walls were candleholders, all different, a bronze glass chimney, an amethyst dish full of floating squat candles, a candelabra dripping with glass icicles. And her loom was there, ready for her, and a basket of wools in all the subtle shades she loved.

In the long days that followed, Fiammarosa found that her husband worked hard, and was no sedentary or sportive prince. Sasania was, he told her, a poor country. The people lived on fish which they caught in the sea, and vegetables irrigated in little plots from the river whose mouth had formed the harbour of the city. Beyond the city, and a few other towns on the coastal strip, Sasan told her, there was nothing but desert – he described dunes and oases, sandstorms and dancing mirages with the passion of a lover describing the woman he loved. Ah, the space of the bare sand, under the sun, under the stars, said Sasan. The taste of dates, of water from deep cool wells. The brilliance of the shimmering unreal cities in the distance, which had given him many ideas for cityscapes and fantastic palaces of glass. Fiammarosa stretched her imagination to conceive what he was describing, and could not. She connected the distant shimmering to her imaginations of lost glaciers and untrodden snowfields. Sasan explained, enthusiastically (they were talking more easily now, though still like two tentative children, not the man and woman whose bodies tangled and fought at night) – Sasan explained the connection of the desert with the glass, which Sasania despatched in trading ships and caravans to the corners of the known world. Glass, Sasan said, was made of the things which they had in abundance – the sand of the desert, three parts, lime, and soda which they made from the wracks, or seaweeds, which clung to the rocks round their coasts. The most difficult, the most precious part, he said, was the wood, which was needed both for the furnaces and for potash. The coastal woods of the country all belonged to the King, and were cared for by rangers. Glass, according to legend, had been found by the first Prince Sasan, who had been no more than an itinerant merchant with a camel train, and had found some lumps and slivers of shining stuff in the cinders of his fire on the seashore. And yet another Sasan had discovered how to blow the molten glass into transparent bottles and bowls, and yet another had discovered how to fuse different colours onto each other. In our country, Sasan said to his wife, princes are glassmakers and glassmakers are princes, and the line of artists runs true in the line of kings.

Every day he brought back from his dark workroom gifts for his bride. He brought crystal balls full of the fused scraps of coloured canes left over from his day's lamp-work. Once, Fiammarosa ventured to the mouth of the cavern where he worked, and peered in. Men stripped to their waists and pouring sweat were feeding the great furnaces, or bending over hot lamps, working on tiny scraps of molten glass with magnifying glasses and sharp tweezers. Others were turning the sullen, cooling red glass with large metal pincers on clattering wheels, and one had a long tube raised to his mouth like a trumpet of doom, blowing his breath into the flaming, molten gob at the end of it which flared and smoked, orange and scarlet, and swelled and swelled. Its hot liquid bursting put the pale princess in mind of the ferocity of her love-making and she opened her mouth, in pleasure and pain, to take in such a blast of hot, sparking wind, that she fell back, and could barely stagger to her room. After that, she spent the long hot days lying on her bed, breathing slowly. Sasan came in the cool of the evening; she took pleasure, then, in food, candle-flames, transparency and shadows. Then they made love. She put it to herself that she was delighting in extremity; that she was living a life pared down to extreme sensations. Dying is an ancient metaphor for the bliss of love, and Fiammarosa died a little, daily. But she was also dying in cold fact. Or in warm fact, to be more precise. She thought she was learning to live for love and beauty, through the power of the will. She was to find that in the end these things are subject to the weather – the weather in the world, and the tourbillons and sluggish meanders of the blood and lymph under the skin.

There was another, growing reason for the sickness against which she threw all her forces. When she understood this, she had a moment of despair and wrote to Hugh, begging him to reconsider his decision. I am not well, she wrote, and the days, as you knew they would be, are long and hot, and I am driven by necessity to languish in inactivity in the dark. I believe I am with child, dear Hugh, and am afraid, in this strange place amongst these strange people, however kind and loving they are. I need your cool head, your wisdom; I need our conversations about history and science. I am *not unhappy*, but I am not well, and I need your counsel, your familiar voice, your good sense. You foresaw that it would be hard – the heat, I mean, the merciless sun, and the confinement which is my only alternative. Could you, best of friends, at least come on a visit?

She despatched this letter, along with her regular letter to her parents, and almost at once regretted it, at least partly. It was a sign of weakness, an appeal for help she should not need. It was as though, by writing down her moment of weakness and discontent, she had made it into a thing, unavoidable. She felt herself becoming weaker and fought against a more and more powerful demon of discontent. Sasan was making her a series of delicate latticino vases. The first was pencil-slender, and took one rose. It was white. The next was cloudy, tinged with pink, and curved slightly outwards. The third was pinker and rounder, the fourth blushed rosy and had a fine blown bowl beneath its narrow neck. When the series of nine was completed, cherry-pink, rose-red, clear-red, deep crimson and almost black with a fiery heart, he arranged them on the table in front of her, and she saw that they were women, each more proudly swollen, with delicate white arms. She smiled, and kissed him, and ignored the fiery choking in her throat.

The next day a letter came from Hugh. It had crossed with her own – she could by no means yet expect an answer. It began with the hope that she would, far away as she was, share his joy, at least in spirit. He had married Hortense, the chamberlain's daughter, and was living in a state of comfort and contentment he had never imagined or hoped for.

There followed, in a riddling form, the only love-letter Fiammarosa had ever had from Hugh. I cannot, he said, hope to live at the extremes of experience, as you can. No one who has ever seen you dance on the untrodden snow, or gather ice-flowers from bare branches, will ever be entirely able to forget this perfect beauty and live with what is pleasant and daily. I see now, said Hugh, that extreme desires extreme, and that beings of pure fire and pure ice may know delights we ordinary mortals must glimpse and forgo. I cannot live in any of your worlds, Princess, and I am happy in my new house, with my pretty woman, who loves me, and my good chair and sprouting garden. But I shall never be *quite* contented, Princess, because I saw you dance in the snow, and the sight took away the possibility of my settling into this life. Be happy in your way, at the furthest edge, and remember, when you can, Hugh, who would be quite happy in his – if he had never seen you.

Fiammarosa wept over this letter. She thought he would not have written so, if it was not meant to be his last letter. She thought, her own letter would cause him pain, and possibly cause him to despise

her, that she could so easily and peremptorily sum-
mon him, when things were hard. And then she
began to weep, because he was not there, and
would not come, and she was alone and sick in a
strange land, where even the cool air in the dark
corridors was warm enough to melt her a little, like
a caress given to a snow figure. When she had wept
some time, she stood up, and began to walk some-
what drunkenly through the long halls and out
across a courtyard full of bright, dazzling air in
which the heat currents could be seen to boil up
and weave their sinuous way down, and up again,
like dry fountains. She went slowly and bravely,
straight across, not seeking the shadow of the
walls, and went into the huge, echoing, cave-like
place where Sasan and his men were at work.
Dimly, dazzled, she saw the half-naked men, the
spinning cocoons, like blazing tulips, on the end of
the pontils, the iron tweezers. Sasan was sitting at
a bench, his dark face illuminated by the red-hot
glow from a still-molten sphere of glass he was
smoothing and turning. Beside him, another
sphere was turning brown, like a dying leaf. One
hand to her belly, Fiammarosa advanced into the

heat and darkness. As she reached Sasan, one of the men, his arms and shoulders running with sweat, his brow dripping, swung open the door of the furnace. Fiammarosa had time to see shelves of forms, red and gold, transparent and burning, before the great sun-like rose of heat and light hit her, and she saw darkness and felt dreadful pain. She was melting, she thought in confusion, as she fell, slowly, slowly, bending and crumpling in the blast, becoming hot and liquid, a white scrap, moaning in a sea of red blood, lit by flames. Sasan was at her side in an instant, his sweat and tears dripping on to the white, cold little face. Before she lost consciousness Fiammarosa heard his small voice, in her head. 'There will be another child, one who would never otherwise have lived; you must think of *that* child.' And then, all was black. There was even an illusion of cold, of shivering.

After the loss of the child, Fiammarosa was ill for a long time. Women covered her brow with cloths soaked in ice-water, changing them assiduously. She lay in the cool and the dark, drifting in and out of a minimal life. Sasan was there, often, sitting silently by her bed. Once, she saw him packing the nine glasses he had made for her in wood-shavings. With care, she recovered, at least enough to become much as she had been in her early days as a girl in her own country, milky, limp and list-less. She rose very late, and sat in her chamber, sipping juice, and making no move to weave, or to read, or to write. After some months, she began to think she had lost her husband's love. He did not come to her bedroom, ever again, after the bloody happening in the furnace-room. He did not speak of this, or explain it, and she could not. She felt she had become a milk-jelly, a blancmange, a Form of a woman, tasteless and unappetising. Because of her metabolism, grief made her fleshier and slower. She wept over the plump rolls of creamy fat around her eyelids, over the bland expanse of her cheeks. Sasan went away on long journeys, and did not say where he was going, or when he would return. She could not write to Hugh, and could not confide in her dark, beautiful attendants. She turned her white face to the dark blue wall, wrapped her soft arms round her body, and wished to die.

Sasan returned suddenly from one of his journeys. It was autumn, or would have been, if there had been any other season than immutable high summer in that land. He came to his wife, and told her to make ready for a journey. They were going to make a journey together, to the interior of his country, he told her, across the desert. Fiammarosa stirred a little in her lethargy.

'I am an icewoman, Sasan,' she said, flatly. 'I cannot survive a journey in the desert.'

'We will travel by night,' he replied. 'We will make shelters for you, in the heat of the day. You will be pleasantly surprised, I trust. Deserts are cold at night. I think you may find it tolerable.'

So they set out, one evening, from the gate of the walled city, as the first star rose in the velvet blue sky. They travelled in a long train of camels and horses. Fiammarosa set out in a litter, slung between mules. As the night deepened, and the fields and the sparse woodlands were left behind, she snuffed a rush of cool air, very pure, coming in from stone and sand, where there was no life, no humidity, no decay. Something lost stirred in her. Sasan rode past, and looked in on her. He told her that they were coming to the dunes, and beyond the first dunes was the true desert. Fiammarosa said she felt well enough to ride beside him, if she might. But he said, not yet, and rode away, in a cloud of dust, white in the moonlight.

And so began a long journey, a journey that took weeks, always by night, under a moon that grew from a pared crescent to a huge silver globe as they travelled. The days were terrible, although Fiammarosa was sheltered by ingenious tents, fanned by servants, cooled with precious water. The nights were clear, empty, and cold. After the first days, Sasan would come for her at dusk, and help her on to a horse, riding beside her, wrapped in a great camel-hair cloak. Fiammarosa shed her layers of protective veiling and rode in a pair of wide white trousers and a flowing shift, feeling the delicious cold run over her skin, bringing it to life, bringing power. She did not ask where they were going. Sasan would tell her when and if he chose to tell her. She did not even wonder why he still did not come to her bed, for the heat of the day made everything, beyond mere survival, impossible. But he spoke to her of the hot desert, of how it was his place. These are the things I am made of, he said, grains of burning sand, and breath of air, and the blaze of light. Like glass. Only here do we see with such clarity. Fiammarosa stared out, sometimes, at the sand as it shimmered in the molten sunlight, and at her husband standing there in the pure heat and emptiness, bathing himself in it. Sometimes, when she looked, there were mirages. Sand and stones appeared to be great lagoons of clear water, great rivers of ice with ice-floes, great forests of conifers. They could have lived together happily, she reflected, by day and night, in these vanishing frozen palaces shining in the hot desert, which became more and more liquid and vanished in strips. But the mirages came and went, and Sasan stood, staring intently at hot emptiness, and Fiammarosa breathed the night air in the cooling sand and plains.

Sometimes, on the horizon, through the rippling glassy air, Fiammarosa saw a mirage which resembled a series of mountain peaks, crowned with white streaks of snow, or feathers of cloud. As they progressed, this vision became more and more steady, less and less shimmering and dissolving. She understood that the mountains were solid, and that their caravan was moving towards them. Those, said Sasan, when she asked, are the Mountains of the Moon. My country has a flat coast, a vast space of desert, and a mountain range which forms the limit of the kingdom. They are barren, inhospitable mountains; not much lives up there; a few eagles, a few rabbits, a kind of ptarmigan. In the past, we were forbidden to go there. It was thought the mountains were the homes of demons. But I have travelled there, many times. He did not say why he was taking Fiammarosa there, and she did not ask.

They came to the foothills, which were all loose scree, and stunted thorn trees. There was a winding narrow path, almost cut into the hills, and they climbed up, and up, partly by day now, for the beasts of burden needed to see their way. Fiammarosa stared upwards with parted lips at the snow on the distant peaks beyond them, as her flesh clung to her damp clothes in the heat. And then suddenly, round a rock, came the entrance to a wide tunnel in the mountainside. They lit torches and lanterns, and went in. Behind them the daylight diminished to a great O and then to a pinprick. It was cooler inside the stone, but not comfortable, for it was airless, and the sense of the weight of the stone above was oppressive. They were travelling inwards and upwards, inwards and upwards, trudging steadily, breathing quietly. And they came, in time, to a great timbered door, on massive hinges. And Sasan put his mouth to a hole beside the keyhole, and blew softly, and everyone could hear a clear musical note, echoed and echoed again, tossed from bell to bell of some unseen carillon. Then the door swung open, lightly and easily, and they went into a place like nowhere Fiammarosa had ever seen.

It was a palace built of glass in the heart of the mountain. They were in a forest of tall glass tubes with branching arms, arranged in colonnades, thickets, circular balustrades. There was a delicate sound in the air, of glass bells, tubular bells, distant waterfalls, or so it seemed. All the glass pillars were hollow, and were filled with columns of liquid – wine-coloured, sapphire, amber, emerald and quicksilver. If you touched the finer ones, the liquid shot up, and then steadied. Other columns held floating glass bubbles, in water, rising and falling, each with a golden numbered weight hanging from its balloon. In the dark antechambers, fantastic candles flowered in glass buds, or shimmered behind shades of figured glass set on ledges and crevices. As they moved onwards through the glass stems, all infinitesimally in motion, they came to a very high chamber miraculously lit by daylight through clear glass in a high funnelled window, far, far above their heads. Here, too, the strange pipes rose upwards, some of them formed like rose bushes, some like carved pillars, some fantastically twined with glass grapes on glass vines. And in this room, there were real waterfalls, sheets of cold water dropping over great slabs of glass, like ice-floes, into glassy pools where it ran away into hidden channels, water falling in sheer fine spray from the rock itself into a huge glass basin, midnight-blue and full of dancing cobalt lights, with a rainbow fountain rising to meet the dancing, descending mare's-tail. All the miracles of invention that glittered and glimmered and trembled could not be taken in at one glance. But Fiammarosa took in one thing. The air was cold.

Cold

By water, by stone, by ice from the mountain top, the air had been chilled to a temperature in which her icewoman's blood stirred to life and her eyes shone.

Sasan showed her further miracles. He showed her her bedchamber, cut into the rock, with its own high porthole window, shaped like a many-coloured rose and with real snow resting on it, far above, so that the light was grainy. Her bed was surrounded by curtains of spun glass, with white birds, snow birds, snowflowers and snow-crystals woven into them. She had her own cooling waterfall, with a controlling gate, to make it greater or smaller, and her own forest of glass trees, with their visible phloem rising and falling. Sasan explained to her the uses of these beautiful inventions, which measured, he said, the weight, the heat, the changes of the ocean of elementary air in which they moved. The rising and falling glass bubbles, each filled to a different weight, measured the heat of the column of water that supported them. The quicksilver columns, in the fine tubes within tubes, were made by immersing the end of the tube in a vessel of mercury, and stopping it with a finger, and then letting the column of quicksilver find its level, at which point the weight of the air could be read off the height of the column in the tube. And this column, he said, varied, with the vapours, the winds, the clouds in the outer atmosphere, with the height above the sea, or the depth of the cavern. You may measure such things also with alcohol, which can be coloured for effect. Fiammarosa had never seen him so animated, nor heard him speak so long. He showed her yet another instrument, which measured the wetness of the incumbent air with the beard of an oat or, in other cases, with a stretched hair. And he had made a system of vents and pulleys, channels and pipes, taps and cisterns, which brought the mountain snow and the deep mountain springs in greater and lesser force into the place, as the barometers and thermometers and hygrometers indicated a need to adjust the air and the temperature. With all these devices, Sasan said, he had made an artificial world, in which he hoped his wife could live, and could breathe, and could be herself, for he could neither bear to keep her in the hot sunny city, nor could he bear to lose her. And Fiammarosa embraced him amongst the sighing spun glass and the whispering water. She could be happy, she said, in all this practical beauty. But what would they live on? How could they survive, on glass, and stone, and water? And Sasan laughed, and took her by the hand, and showed her great chambers in the rock where all sorts of plants were growing, under windows which had been cut to let in the sun, and glazed to adjust his warmth, and where runnels of water ran between fruit trees and seedlings, pumpkin plants and herbs. There was even a cave for a flock of goats, hardy and silky, who went out to graze on the meagre pastures and came in at night. He himself must come and go, Sasan said, for he had his work, and his land to look to. But she would be safe here, she could breathe, she could live in her own way, or almost, he said, looking anxiously at her. And she assured him that she would be more than happy there. 'We can make air, water, light, into something both of us can live in,' said Sasan. 'All I know, and some things I have had to invent, has gone into building this place for you.'

But the best was to come. When it was night, and the whole place was sleeping, with its cold air currents moving lazily between the glass stems, Sasan came to Fiammarosa's room, carrying a lamp, and a narrow package, and said, 'Come with me.' So she followed him, and he led her to a rocky stairway that went up, and round, and up, and round, until it opened on the side of the mountain itself, above the snow-line. Fiammarosa stepped out under a black velvet sky, full of burning cold silver stars, like globes of mercury, on to a field of untouched snow, such as she had never thought to see again. And she took off her slippers and stepped out on to the sparkling crust, feeling the delicious crackle beneath her toes, the soft sinking, the voluptuous cold. Sasan opened his packet, which contained the strange flute he had played when he wooed her. He looked at his wife, and began to play, a lilting, swaying tune that ran away over the snowfields and whispered into the edges of silence. And Fiammarosa took off her dress, and her shawls and her petticoat, stood naked in the snow, shook out her pale hair and began to dance. As she danced, a whirling white shape, her skin of ice-crystals, that she had believed she would never feel again, began to form along her veins, over her breasts, humming round her navel. She was lissom and sparkling, she was cold to the bone and full of life. The moon glossed the snow with gold and silver. When, finally, Sasan stopped playing, the icewoman darted over to him, laughing with delight, and discovered that his lips and fingers were blue with cold; he had stopped because he could play no more. So she rubbed his hands with her cold hands, and kissed his mouth with her cold lips, and with friction and passion brought his blood back to some movement. They went back to the bedchamber with the spun-glass curtains, and opened and closed a few channels and conduits, and lay down to make love in a mixture of currents of air, first warm, then cooling, which brought both of them to life.

In a year, or so, twin children were born, a dark boy, who resembled his mother at birth, and became, like her, pale and golden, and a pale, flower-like girl, whose first days were white and hairless, but who grew a mane of dark hair like her father's and had a glass-blower's, flute-player's mouth. And if Fiammarosa was sometimes lonely in her glass palace, and sometimes wished both that Sasan would come more often, and that she could roam amongst fjords and ice-fells, this was not unusual, for no one has everything she can desire. But she was resourceful and hopeful, and made a study of the vegetation of the Sasanian snow-line, and a further study of which plants could thrive in mountain air under glass windows, and corresponded – at long intervals – with authorities all over the world on these matters. Her greatest discovery was a sweet blueberry, that grew in the snow, but in the glass garden became twice the size, and almost as delicate in flavour.

Baglady

Composition, Darren Haggar, 1998

Baglady

'And then,' says Lady Scroop brightly, 'the Company will send cars to take us all to the Good Fortune Shopping Mall. I understand that it is a real Aladdin's Cave of Treasures, where we can all find prezzies for everyone and all sorts of little indulgences for ourselves, and in perfect safety: the entrances to the Mall are under constant surveillance, sad, but necessary in these difficult days.'

Daphne Gulver-Robinson looks round the breakfast table. It is beautifully laid with peach-coloured damask, bronze cutlery, and little floating gardens in lacquered dishes of waxy flowers that emit gusts of perfume. The directors of Doolittle Wind Quietus are in a meeting. Their wives are breakfasting together under the eye of Lady Scroop, the chairman's wife. It is Lord Scroop's policy to encourage his directors to travel with their wives. Especially in the Far East, and especially since the figures about AIDS began to be drawn to his attention.

Most of the wives are elegant, with silk suits and silky legs and exquisitely cut hair. They chat mutedly, swapping recipes for chutney and horror stories about nannies, staring out of the amber glass wall of the Precious Jade Hotel at the dimpling sea. Daphne Gulver-Robinson is older than most of them, and dowdier, although her husband, Rollo, has less power than most of the other directors. She has tried to make herself attractive for this jaunt and has lost ten pounds and had her hands manicured; but now she sees the other ladies, she knows it is not enough. Her style is seated tweed, and stout shoes, and bird's-nest hair.

'You don't want me on this trip,' she said to Rollo when told about it. 'I'd better stay and mind the donkeys and the geese and the fantails as usual, and you can have a good time, as usual, in those exotic places.'

'Of course I don't want you,' said Rollo. 'That is, of course I *want* you, but I do know you're happier with the geese and the donkeys and pigs and things. But Scroop will think it's very odd, *I'm* very odd, if you don't come. He gets bees in his bonnet. You'll like the shopping; the ladies do a lot of shopping, I believe. You might like the other wives,' he finished, not hopefully.

'I didn't like boarding-school,' Daphne said.

'I don't see what that has to do with it,' Rollo said. There is a lot Rollo doesn't see. Doesn't want to see and doesn't see.

Lady Scroop tells them they may scatter in the Mall as much as they like as long as they are all back at the front entrance at noon precisely. 'We have all *packed our bags*, I hope,' she says, 'though I have left time on the schedule for adjustments to make space for any goodies we may find. And then there will be a *delicious lunch* at the Pink Pearl Café and then we leave at two-forty-five *sharp* for the airport and on to Sydney.'

The ladies pack into the cars. Daphne Gulver-Robinson is next to the driver of her Daimler, a place of both comfort and isolation. They swoop silently through crowded streets, isolated by bullet-proof glass from the smells and sounds of the Orient. The Mall is enormous and not beautiful. Some of the ladies have been in post-modern

pink and peppermint Malls in San Diego, some
have been in snug, glittering underground tunnels
in Canadian winters, some have shopped in crystal
palaces in desert landscapes, with tinkling fountains and splashing streams. The Good Fortune
Shopping Mall resembles an army barracks or a
prison block, but it is not for the outside they have
come, and they hasten to trip inside, like hens
looking for worms, jerking and clucking, Daphne
Gulver-Robinson thinks malevolently, as none of
them waits for her.

She synchronises her watch with the driver, and
goes in alone, between the sleepy soldiers with
machine-guns and the uniformed police with their
revolvers and little sticks. Further away, along the
walls of the Mall, are little groups and gangs of
human flotsam and jetsam, gathered with bags and
bottles around little fires of cowdung or card-
board. There is a no-man's-land, swept clean,
between them and the police.

She is not sure she likes shopping. She looks at
her watch, and wonders how she will fill the two
hours before the rendezvous. She walks rather
quickly past rows of square shop-fronts, glittering

with gilt and silver, shining with pearls and opals, shimmering with lacquer and silk. Puppets and shadow-puppets mop and mow, paper birds hop on threads, paper dragons and monstrous goldfish gape and dangle. She covers the first floor, or one rectangular arm of the first floor, ascends a flight of stairs and finds herself on another floor, more or less the same, except for a few windows full of sober suiting, a run of American-style T-shirts, an area of bonsai trees. She stops to look at the trees, remembering her garden, and thinks of buying a particularly shapely cherry. But how could it go to Sydney, how return to Norfolk, would it even pass customs?

She has slowed down now and starts looking. She comes to a corner, gets into a lift, goes up, gets out, finds herself on a higher, sunnier, emptier floor. There are fewer shoppers. She walks along one whole 'street' where she is the only shopper, and is taken by a display of embroidered silk cushion-covers. She goes in, and turns over a heap of about a hundred, quick, quick, chrysanthemums, cranes, peach-blossom, blue-tits, mountain tops. She buys a cover with a circle of embroidered fish, red and gold and copper, because it is the only one of its kind, perhaps a rarity. When she looks in her shopping bag, she cannot find her camera, although she is sure it was there when she set out. She buys a jade egg on the next floor, and some lacquered chopsticks, and a mask with a white furious face for her student daughter. She is annoyed to see a whole window full of the rare fishes, better embroidered than the one in the bag. She follows a sign saying CAFÉ but cannot find the café, though she trots on, faster now. She does find a ladies' room, with cells so small they are hard to squeeze into. She restores her make-up there: she looks hot and blowzy. Her lipstick has bled into the soft skin round her mouth. Hairpins have sprung out. Her nose and eyelids shine. She looks at her watch, and thinks she should be making her way back to the entrance. Time has passed at surprising speed.

Signs saying EXIT appear with great frequency and lead to fire-escape-like stairways and lifts, which debouch only in identical streets of boxed shop-fronts. They are designed, she begins to think, to keep you inside, to direct you past even more shops, in search of a hidden, deliberately elusive way out. She runs a little, trotting quicker, toiling up concrete stairways, clutching her shopping. On one of these stairways a heel breaks off one of her smart shoes. After a moment she takes off both, and puts them in her shopping bag. She hobbles on, on the concrete, sweating and panting. She dare not look at her watch, and then does. The time of the rendezvous is well past. She thinks she might call the hotel, opens her handbag, and finds that her purse and credit cards have mysteriously disappeared.

There is nowhere to sit down: she stands in the Mall, going through and through her handbag, long after it is clear that the things have vanished. Other things, dislodged, have to be retrieved from the dusty ground. Her fountain-pen has gone too, Rollo's present for their twentieth wedding anniversary. She begins to run quite fast, so that huge holes spread in the soles of her stockings, which in the end split, and begin to work their way over her feet and up her legs in wrinkles like flaking skin. She looks at her watch; the packing-time and the 'delicious lunch' are over: it is almost time for the airport car. Her bladder is bursting, but she *must go on*, and must go *down*, the entrance is down.

It is in this way that she discovers that the Good Fortune Mall extends maybe as far into the earth as into the sky, excavated identical caverns of shop-fronts, jade, gold, silver, silk, lacquer, watches, suiting, bonsai trees and masks and puppets. Lifts that say they are going down go only up. Stairwells are windowless: ground level cannot be found. The plane has now taken off with or without the directors and ladies of Doolittle Wind Quietus. She takes time out in another concrete and stainless-steel lavatory cubicle, and then looks at the watch, whose face has become a whirl of terror. Only now it is merely a compressed circle of pink skin, shiny with sweat. Her watch, too, has gone. She utters faint little moaning sounds, and then an experimental scream. No one appears to hear or see her, neither strolling shoppers, deafened by Walkmans or by propriety, or by fear of the strange, nor shopkeepers, watchful in their cells.

Nevertheless, screaming helps. She screams again, and then screams and screams into the thick, bustling silence. A man in a brown overall brings a policeman in a reinforced hat, with a gun and a stick.

'Help me,' says Daphne. 'I am an English lady, I have been robbed, I must get home.'

'Papers,' says the policeman.

She looks in the back pocket of her handbag. Her passport, too, has gone. There is nothing. 'Stolen. All stolen,' she says.

'People like you,' says the policeman, 'not allowed in here.'

She sees herself with his eyes, a baglady, dirty, unkempt, with a bag full of somebody's shopping, a tattered battery-hen.

'My husband will come and look for me,' she tells the policeman.

If she waits, if she stays in the Mall, he will, she thinks. He *must*. She sees herself sitting with the flotsam and jetsam beyond the swept no-man's-land, outside.

'I'm not moving,' she says, and sits down heavily. She has to stay in the Mall. The policeman prods her with his little stick.

'Move, please.'

It is more comfortable sitting down.

'I shall stay here for ever if necessary,' she says.

She cannot imagine anyone coming. She cannot imagine getting out of the Good Fortune Mall.

Jael

Jael and Sisera, School of Rembrandt

Jael

I remember very clearly, Mrs Hodges said, 'What a lovely colour, Jess,' and I spread it further and further across the page of the Scripture book. If you got five As in a row, you got sent to the head-mistress to be congratulated, and I had got as far as four, though none of us thought Scripture counted, compared to English, or History, or Science. It was a lovely colour, it was a true ver-milion, and I spread it and spread it, all over the page. I had a good box of pencils, about twenty-four colours, including some unusual pinks and turquoises. You could get quite convincing flesh colours with those pencils, but I wasn't much good at drawing. In fact, I had made Jael's headdress fall forward over her face, and concentrated on her arm and the hammer, and the tent-peg, and the great sheet of blood stemming out like a great river into a sheet, or a cloth, over the couch he lay on, and the floor of Jael's tent, and the greyish, over-absorbent lined page of my exercise book. I don't really think I asked myself at the time why we were being asked to illustrate this very odd tale. I really don't think so. Nor do I really think there is any reason why I remember that drawing more than any other in that exercise book. I can't, for instance, remember what I got the four As for, or even whether I got an A for my rendering of Jael's neat and bloody disposal of Sisera. I wasn't particularly trying to please Mrs Hodges, who was not religious, she was a history teacher doing her stint at Scripture, as most of them did. Scripture didn't have important teachers, either, and got shared out as a chore. She was unusual, in those days (the early 1950s), for being married. She had a lot of long curly dark hair, and red lips, and wickedly pointed very high heels, on which she clipped along between our desks. Youngish, for a teacher at that good, ancient establishment for girls. Not a good teacher, you remember those. I am quite sure, though I don't remember a word she did say, that she gave us no explanation of why we had to study and illustrate that peculiarly disagreeable and morally equivocal story. Anyway, for some reason, the experience of making that pool of red with my good pencil on the bad paper has stayed with me. I was telling the cameraman in the studio in Brussels about it, over lunch. We were talking about how your past life is mapped two ways, with significant things that of course you remember, births, marriages, deaths, journeys, successes and failures, and then the other sort, the curiously bright-coloured, detailed pointless moments that won't go away. He's in his early thirties, he looked a bit sorry for me, when I told him about Jael, that I was old enough to have memories so far back. So small and bright and faraway, like illuminations in manuscripts. We discussed the horrible story, and he was very struck by it. (He had a completely religion-free upbringing, I don't think he ever opened a Bible in his life.) I said, and I'm sure I'm right, that I didn't think I was remembering it for its shocking morals, I said I was sure I was remembering it because of the excitement I'd felt over spreading more and more of that red over the paper. Like the blown-up-and-up shot we used in the Spanaranja commercial, all those glistening exploding sacs lying together in a segment of a blood orange. You didn't get much intense sensuous excitement at Armadale High School, Girls' Public Day School Trust, GPDST.

Anyway, that caused me to think, not for the first time, about Jael and Sisera. I'm sure all those Scripture stories we did at the ages of nine and ten are the reason I find religion not only incredible, but disgusting and dangerous. At that stage, you're already doing bits of Shakespeare, at least at the kind of segregated high-powered school I was at, and even if you say, or believe, you're bored or indifferent, there are all those passionate people, all those complicated motives, all that singing language, all the power, and, later, you know it changed you for ever. But the Scriptures were both dead and nasty. And all we did was illustrate them, frame by frame, the Coat of Many Colours, the Manna in the Wilderness, the Plagues, Jael and Sisera.

Explaining it to Jed, our cameraman, I said, it's not even a story about treachery or loyalty. I told it him from memory, as it came into my head whenever I saw that red sheet. It happens in the Book of Judges, when the Judge, unusually, is a woman,

Deborah. (No, we were not offered her as a rôle-model for leadership qualities. I'm not sure the concept existed in the early 1950s. If it did, she wasn't it, more likely Florence Nightingale or Elizabeth Fry.) The Israelites as usual had done evil in the sight of the Lord who sold them into the hands of Jabin, King of Canaan, whose captain, Sisera, mightily oppressed them with nine hundred chariots of iron for twenty years. Then Deborah traps Sisera in the river of Kishon. The Bible says 'The Lord discomfited Sisera and all his chariots, and all his host, with the edge of the sword.' The Lord did his own killing at that point of the Bible, but Deborah organised it. Sisera got out of his chariot, and fled away on his feet, and came to the tent of Jael, the wife of Heber the Kenite, who was at peace with Sisera's King Jabin. And Jael said to Sisera, 'Turn in, my lord, turn in to me; fear not.' And he went in, and when he asked for water, she opened a bottle of milk, and covered him, and invited him to rest. And he asked her to stand in the door of the tent, and say no man had come that way. The next bit I have always known by heart.

'Then Jael Heber's wife took a nail of the tent, and took an hammer in her hand, and went softly unto him, and smote the nail into his temples, and fastened it into the ground: for he was fast asleep and weary. So he died.'

Now I think about it, it's a story about the breaking of all the primitive laws of hospitality, and kindness, laws we learn even from fairy-stories. Jael was not Sisera's enemy; she enticed him in, and gratuitously betrayed him. The next chapter of the Bible (Judges 5) is Deborah's song of triumph. It is full of amazing rhythms, in the King James Bible. It is a nasty piece of work. Listen.

Blessed above women shall Jael the wife of Heber the Kenite be, blessed shall she be above women in the tent.

He asked water, and she gave him milk; she brought forth butter in a lordly dish.

She put her hand to the nail, and her right hand to the workmen's hammer; and with the hammer she smote Sisera, she smote off his head, when she had pierced and stricken through his temples.

At her feet he bowed, he fell, he lay down: at her feet he bowed, he fell; where he bowed, there he fell down dead.

The mother of Sisera looked out at a window, and cried through the lattice, Why is his chariot so long in coming? why tarry the wheels of his chariots?

Her wise ladies answered her, yea, she returned answer to herself,

Have they not sped? have they not divided the prey; to every man a damsel or two; to Sisera a prey of divers colours, a prey of divers colours of needlework, of divers colours of needlework on both sides, meet for the necks of them that take the spoil?

So let all thine enemies perish, O LORD.

I love the rhythms of that. I love to think of those seventeenth-century bishops, in a world where bishops were regularly burned for believing, or not believing, things, making those rhythms. At her feet he bowed, he fell, he lay down; at her feet he bowed, he fell; where he bowed, there he fell down dead. I don't know what

Hebrew rhythm they were echoing, but the English is done with heavy monosyllables, strokes of the hammer, strokes of the axe, and yet it flows, too. All those rhythms and phrases are vanishing from our world. My mother, every time she opened the fridge, would say, 'Here is the butter in a lordly dish,' and when I found it in the Bible, it was a piece fitting into a cultural jigsaw. It is a long time ago. The fridge was our first, and very new. In the war, our milk and butter were in earthenware pots under wet muslin veils, weighted with little heavy clay beads, red and blue.

When I did the Grenadine commercial, I made a red silk tent that made great pools of red light on a glittery sandy floor. The politically incorrect desert warrior poured the crimson juice from a kind of Venetian claret jug. There was a lordly dish on a low table, with a great swirling pyramid of something creamy that caught the pink light. Lara, who is my assistant director and wants my job, says you can't make images like that any more. People have the wrong associations to desert warriors and captive pale maidens. She just looked blank when I told her that I'd also been playing with the image of Persephone, eating pomegranate seeds in the underworld, with dusky-skinned gloomy Dis. I had a lovely plate of the seeds, too, another richer, if less lordly, dish, next to the buttery stuff, little bits of pink jelly, glistening. I shouldn't have told her about Persephone; it convinced her even more that I'm *passé*, in need of replacement, encumbered with dead cultural baggage. I might have done better to tell her about my other idea, about hand grenades being called grenades, like Grenadine, because they resemble pomegranates, in shape, and in being full of explosive seeds. What a delicious metaphor, sheets of red juice, explosions of extreme sensuality, sheets of red blood. Attached to nothing, it's just the quirky way my mind works. I got a First at Cambridge, writing Empsonian essays unpacking complicated multiple metaphors. Unpacking's a more modern word, we didn't use it then, you could make a film where you opened a velvet ball and floods of red silk and light filled the screen – what would you use that for? It's odd to be a pointless poet who doesn't make poems, only commercials for fruit drinks. I enjoy that. It's never dull. Lately it's become a bit frightening.

Anyway, Jael. Why do I remember Jael? Metaphors. I do know – I have always known – that I felt a faint click of symmetry as I drove the point of my pencil into the paper. Pencil, peg. Another *detached* image, like the grenade. Pointed. Pointless. I do know also that whenever I remember that patch of fierce colour I remember, like an after-image, a kind of dreadful murky colour, a yellow-khaki-mustard-*thick* colour, that is the colour of the days of our boredom. For we were not unhappy girls, we were cared-for, nice, clever girls, and we were bored. It's quite hard to think back to that time. All the buildings were the same colours, green and cream. We wore milk-chocolate-coloured gymslips over khaki-coloured shirts, with what we then amiably called nigger-brown ties. I do not believe any of us thought of the nasty meaning of those words, nigger-brown, we just recognised the colour. Ignorance, inno-cence, boredom. It's strange how I hesitate, out of fear, to write down the true fact that we used that word, in that unloaded way. It's so long ago, we shall be judged without being imagined. All the excitement of life was in books. Jane Eyre, with her burning bed-curtains, or being punished in the Red Room (I've made films with both those images, fire insurance and children's furniture). Ivanhoe charging, Robin Hood in the dappled green light with his bow, Eliza escaping across the breaking ice, wolves and narwhals, volcanoes and tidal waves, excitement was all in books, none of it, nothing at all, seeped out into life. We were the pre-television age, and we cannot – that is, the absolute quality of our boredom cannot – be imagined by those who grew up with the magic lantern, the magic window on the world, the Pandora's box peopling the world with temptations and emotions and *knowledge* and other places and people in the corner of the lounge/sitting room/front room. I know young people now have a worked-up nostalgia for an imaginary time when families communicated, people made things, played games, instead of passively watching. Now and then we did. I remember the physical pleasure of frenzied playground skipping. I remember the passionate

life with which I invested a collection of lead
ponies. But mostly – apart from books – I remember this smeared, fuggy, limited light of
boredom, where you couldn't see very much or
very far, and the horizon was unimaginable.

Human beings are human beings, Lara and the
cameramen might say. You must have had loves
and hatreds, friends and enemies, then, as now. We
did have gangs. We had two gangs, in our class, to
be precise. They were called, unimaginatively,
after their 'leaders'. One was Wendy's gang, and
the other was Rachel's gang. Wendy's gang was
bigger, because Wendy was the most popular girl
in the class, which was surprising, perhaps, since
she was also both the cleverest girl and the best at
sports, more or less. She came top in English, and
top in Maths (and top in Scripture, as far as I can
remember – Scripture, as I said, didn't count). She
won races, particularly long-distance ones, particularly the junior school cross-country run. Wendy
was good-looking in a completely inoffensive,
unexceptionable way. She had honey-blonde hair,
blue eyes, a broad brow, a wide mouth. She was
tall, but not too tall, she was developing into a

woman, but not awkwardly. She was a *nice* girl. It wasn't fair that she should have everything, and be nice with it, but that was how it was. She was the person in the parable of the talents who was given ten talents and industriously made another ten talents. (Did I see myself as the servant with the one talent, who hid it in the earth in case it got stolen?) Rachel was dark, and sinewy, good too at games but not at all in Wendy's class as an academic high-flyer. Rachel had deep-set brown eyes, and straight black plaits, and long fine hands, and an indefinable sexiness, nothing to do with puberty. It was Wendy who had the beginnings of breasts. Rachel was thin and wiry. Wendy was going to pass the eleven-plus into the senior school with no problem, whereas Rachel's future was uncertain, and she showed a mild sulky rebelliousness to the teachers. I should think Rachel's gang was about a third the size of Wendy's. The girls in it were naughtier, less conformist. In the context, you must understand, of our all being totally respectable nice girls.

Wendy's gang, at playtime, sat around on the low stone wall round the netball courts and

Rachel's gang met in the bushes, in the sooty Victorian laurel-bushes near the gate into the school grounds.

I think, looking back, that Rachel had leadership qualities, and that Wendy didn't – she was simply too agreeable, her gang clustered round her because she was a star whose star quality was a perfect normality. Looking back, I think you could call it grace. She did things – things she was asked to do, things she was expected to do, things she mildly liked to do – as well as she could, and was briefly surprised to find that no one else could do them anywhere near as well. Whereas Rachel was moody. You had to be on the right side of her, or she picked on you. No, I can't remember any instance of her picking on anyone, nothing so precise. Just an atmosphere, a smoke, of possible danger.

There was a fringe of girls, like myself, who hung around the edges of the gangs, not sure if we were admitted as members or not. Because we weren't sure, we were also uncertain what the gangs *did*. What was being discussed, in secret whispers, in smuggled notes in Scripture lessons, in the bogs. We thought, if we could be in the inner circle – both gangs had an inner circle of about four or five acolytes and the Leader – we would be part of something that was going on, we would be less bored.

I know now, I know the secret of what was going on. It was nothing at all. Or at least, all that was going on was the self-perpetuation of the structure of the gangs, the inner circles, the outer circles, the tension between Wendy's gang in the sun and Rachel's in the shade. We were in a green suburb of an industrial town, and when we crossed the town, on winter afternoons, to go home to tea, we saw *real* gangs, that is, active gangs, boys with bicycle chains, boys with knives and heavy boots, boys whose doings were reported in the papers, sometimes. We hurried past, looking unfrightened, walking together, safety in numbers. But our gangs were not *gangs*. Nothing ever happened.

Or at least, I think nothing happened. No, change that, *something* happened, but I do not remember how.

I had the idea, because I read so many books, that treachery would make the gangs interesting. A girl could betray the secrets of one gang to the other, if she could find any secrets to betray. I think I was interested in treachery because of the charm of Rupert of Hentzau. I hadn't met that other charmer, Edmund in *King Lear*, I'm fairly sure. I may have hit on some narrative universal: what is interesting about boring gangs has to be treachery. It was a silly idea, because, as I said, there were no secrets, no plans of battle, no battles, nothing to betray. I watch Lara betraying me with all the inventiveness of her, our, fraught and hyperactive trade, and I look back on the innocent child I was, with my dreams of drama, with a sad pity. Our world is full of a buzz about surveys which have been commissioned which show that *one boring commercial* can lose the audience for the whole commercial break round it, can even diminish the audience for the television programme into which our break breaks. She is putting it about, in whispers, that another soft-drinks firm has done a survey that shows that both my Spanaranja and my Grenadine films are infecting whole slots with boredom and apathy. I think, myself, she invented not only the findings, but the survey. It was, I have to admit, a resourceful idea, which will leave a question hanging like smoke in the atmosphere, even if I manage to get rid of the survey or demolish its hypothesised findings. She's quick, and she's brave. She lives in a world of interactive computer-generated gladiators, bomb-lobbers, kamikaze scantily clad dolls, headsmen with swords and laser-duellists my reactions aren't quick enough for. She can fill screens with blood I shall drown in, at the touch of her glossy black fingernails.

I did have another idea, I think, about Wendy and Rachel. I thought, if some girl stretched a dark cord across the path, in the cross-country run, she could bring down Wendy in her pride as she strode past, leaving the way clear for Rachel, who would be impressed and grateful. It would be a *real* secret, something would really have happened, that could never be told. It would be real treachery, not just giggling and whispering. Rachel would be able to recognise the degree of difference, between talk and something really happening, for once. I didn't have this idea, particularly, because I was in love with Rachel and hated Wendy. Or the other way round, because I was in love with Wendy, and she spurned me for her inner circle. She never exactly spurned anyone – her inner circle got there through the greater persistence of their greater desire. I don't think I was in love with either of them, or with anyone, except Sir Lancelot, and Rupert, and Saladin, and Mr Rochester. I was afraid of being annihilated by boredom, of there never being anything else. Once I thought about talking to Rachel about my idea about the cord, of course, I saw how impossible the idea was. She wouldn't have listened, and might have reacted quite nastily, or been put off, or even scared. The scenario of her secret gratitude was just that – a tenuous scenario, and I abandoned it. I was sorry, because I knew where the good place to stretch the cord would be, between the trees in a copse on the climb round the rough scree near the old quarry. There was cover for the traitor to retrieve the cord, and get away, in the confusion. The traitor would be dressed for the race, but would have skipped a large part of the circuit, cutting straight through the trees.

The thing that happened was, that Wendy,

running easily, and well ahead of everyone else, did stumble and fall, in exactly that place. She fell quite a way, down the scree, and hit her head very nastily on a sharp stone, and broke a vertebra and a rib, and was in hospital for quite a long time. She was unconscious for quite a long time, too, and when she did come round was, to use a cliché which is conveniently to hand, 'never the same again'. A light went out. She took the eleven-plus with the rest of us, and didn't pass. Neither did Rachel, or not to our very superior school, and after a time I heard no more of either of them. I don't know what became of Wendy after the Secondary Modern. I have a very clear memory of the piece of cord – sort of fairly thick garden twine, such as my father had in his shed, a dark khaki-green twine, completely invisible over dead leaves and puddles. I have the opposite of Alzheimer's, I remember things I really think didn't happen. After all, my job is scenarios, is finding props, is imagining lighting, the figure entering the frame, and ACTION. I remember Jael because the story doesn't quite make sense, the emotions are all in a muddle, you are asked to rejoice in wickedness. I remember Jael because of the delicious red, because of the edge of excitement in wielding the pencil-point, because I had a half-a-glimpse of making art and colour.

Christis in the House of
Martha and Mary

Kitchen Scene with Christ in the House of Martha and Mary
(detail), Diego Velázquez, c. 1618

Christ in the House of
Martha and Mary

Cooks are notoriously irascible. The new young woman, Dolores, was worse than most, Concepción thought. Worse and better, that was. She had an extraordinary fine nose for savours and spices, and a light hand with pastries and batters, despite her stalwart build and her solid arms. She could become a true artist, if she chose, she could go far. But she didn't know her place. She sulked, she grumbled, she complained. She appeared to think it was by some sort of unfortunate accident that she had been born a daughter of servants, and not a delicate lady like Doña Conchita who went to church in sweeping silks and a lace veil. Concepción told Dolores, not without an edge of unkindness, that she wouldn't look so good in those clothes, anyway. You are a mare built for hard work, not an Arab filly, said Concepción. You are no beauty. You are all brawn, and you should thank God for your good health in the station to which he has called you. Envy is a deadly sin.

It isn't envy, said Dolores. I want to live. I want time to think. Not to be pushed around. She studied her face in a shining copper pan, which exaggerated the heavy cheeks, the angry pout. It was true she was no beauty, but no woman likes being told so. God had made her heavy, and she hated him for it.

The young artist was a friend of Concepción's. He borrowed things, a pitcher, a bowl, a ladle, to sketch them over and over. He borrowed Concepción, too, sitting quietly in a corner, under the hooked hams and the plaits of onions and garlic, and drawing her face. He made Concepción look, if not ideally beautiful, then wise and grace- ful. She had good bones, a fine mouth, a wonderful pattern of lines on her brow, and etched beside her nose, which Dolores had not been interested in until she saw the shapes he made from them. His sketches of Concepción increased her own know- ledge that she was not beautiful. She never spoke to him, but worked away in a kind of fury in his presence, grinding the garlic in the mortar, filleting the fish with concentrated skill, slapping dough, making a tattoo of sounds with the chopper, like hailstones, reducing onions to fine specks of translucent light. She felt herself to be a heavy space of unregarded darkness, a weight of miserable shadow in the corners of the room he was abstractedly recording. He had given Concepción an oil painting he had made, of shining fish and white solid eggs, on a chipped earthenware dish. Dolores did not know why this painting moved her. It was silly that oil paint on board should make eggs and fish more real, when they were less so. But it did. She never spoke to him, though she partly knew that if she did, he might in the end give her some small similar patch of light in darkness to treasure.

Sunday was the worst day. On Sunday, after Mass, the family entertained. They entertained family and friends, the priest and sometimes the bishop and his secretary, they sat and conversed, and Doña Conchita turned her dark eyes and her pale, long face to listen to the Fathers, as they made kindly jokes and severe pronouncements on the state of the nation, and of Christendom. There were not enough servants to keep up the flow of sweetmeats and pasties, syllabubs and jellies, quails and tartlets, so that Dolores was sometimes needed to fetch and carry as well as serve, which she did with an ill grace. She did not cast her eyes modestly down, as was expected, but stared around her angrily, watching the convolutions of Doña Conchita's neck with its pretty necklace, the tapping of her pretty foot, directed not at the padre whose words she was demurely attending to, but at young Don José on the other side of the room. Dolores put a hot dish of peppers in oil down on the table with such force that the pottery burst apart, and oil and spices ran into the damask cloth. Doña Ana, Doña Conchita's governess, berated Dolores for a whole minute, threatening dismissal, docking of wages, not only for clumsiness but for insolence. Dolores strode back into the kitchen, not slinking, but moving her large legs like walking oak trees, and began to shout. There was no need to dismiss her, she was off. This was no life for a human being. She was no worse than *they* were, and more of use. She was off.

The painter was in his corner, eating her dish of

elvers and *alioli*. He addressed her directly for the first time, remarking that he was much in her debt, over these last weeks, for her good nose for herbs, for her tact with sugar and spice, for her command of sweet and sour, rich and delicate. You are a true artist, said the painter, gesturing with his fork.

Dolores turned on him. He had no right to mock her, she said. He was a true artist, he could reveal light and beauty in eggs and fishes that no one had seen, and which they would then always see. She made pastries and dishes that went out of the kitchen beautiful and came back mangled and mashed – they don't notice what they're eating, they're so busy talking, and they don't eat most of it, in case they grow fat, apart from the priests, who have no other pleasures. They order it all for show, for show, and it lasts a minute only until they put the knife to it, or push it around their plate elegantly with a fork.

The painter put his head on one side, and considered her red face as he considered the copper jugs, or the glassware, narrowing his eyes to a slit. He asked her if she knew the story St Luke told, of Christ in the house of Martha and Mary. No, she said, she did not. She knew her catechism, and what would happen to sinners at the Last Judgment, which was on the wall of the church. And about butchered martyrs, who were also on the walls of the church.

They were sisters, the painter told her, who lived in Bethany. Jesus visited them, from time to time, and rested there. And Mary sat at his feet and listened to his words, and Martha was cumbered with much serving, as St Luke put it, and complained. She said to the Lord, 'Dost thou not care that my sister hath left me to serve alone? bid her therefore that she help me.' And Jesus said to her, 'Martha, Martha, thou art careful and troubled about many things: but one thing is needful, and Mary hath chosen that good part, which shall not be taken away from her.'

Dolores considered this, drawing her brows together in an angry frown. She said, 'There speaks a man, for certain. There will always be serving, and someone will always be doomed to serving, and will have no choice or chance about the *better part*. Our Lord could make loaves and fishes from the air for the listeners, but mere mortals cannot.

So we – Concepción and I – serve them whilst they have the *better part* they have chosen.'

And Concepción said that Dolores should be careful, or she would be in danger of blaspheming. She should learn to accept the station the Lord had given her. And she appealed to the painter, should Dolores not learn to be content, to be patient? Hot tears sprang in Dolores's eyes. The painter said:

'By no means. It is not a question of accepting our station in the world as men have ordered it, but of learning not to be careful and troubled. Dolores here has her way to that better part, even as I have, and, like mine, it begins in attention to loaves and fishes. What matters is not that silly girls push her work about their plates with a fork, but that the work is good, that she understands what the wise understand, the nature of garlic and onions, butter and oil, eggs and fish, peppers, aubergines, pumpkins and corn. The cook, as much as the painter, looks into the essence of the creation, not, as I do, in light and on surfaces, but with all the other senses, with taste, and smell, and touch, which God also made in us for purposes. You may come at the *better part* by understanding emulsions, Dolores, by studying freshness and the edges of decay in leaves and flesh, by mixing wine and blood and sugar into sauces, as well as I may, and likely better than fine ladies twisting their pretty necks so that the light may catch their pretty pearls. You are very young, Dolores, and very strong, and very angry. You must learn *now*, that the important lesson – as long as you have your health – is that the divide is not between the servants and the served, between the leisured and the workers, but between those who are *interested* in the world and its multiplicity of forms and forces, and those who merely subsist, worrying or yawning. When I paint eggs and fishes and onions, I am painting the godhead – not only because eggs have been taken as an emblem of the Resurrection, as have dormant roots with green shoots, not only because the letters of Christ's name make up the Greek word for fish, but because the world is full of light and life, and the true crime is not to be interested in it. You have a way in. Take it. It may incidentally be a way out, too, as all skills are. The Church teaches that Mary is the contemplative life, which is higher than

Martha's way, which is the active way. But any painter must question, which is which? And a cook also contemplates mysteries.'

'I don't know,' said Dolores, frowning. He tilted his head the other way. Her head was briefly full of images of the skeletons of fishes, of the whirlpool of golden egg-and-oil in the bowl, of the pattern of muscles in the shoulder of a goat. She said, 'It is nothing, what I know. It is past in a flash. It is cooked and eaten, or it is gone bad and fed to the dogs, or thrown out.'

'Like life,' said the painter. 'We eat and are eaten, and we are very lucky if we reach our three score years and ten, which is less than a flash in the eyes of an angel. The understanding persists, for a time. In your craft and mine.'

He said, 'Your frown is a powerful force in itself. I have an idea for a painting of Christ in the house of Martha and Mary. Would you let me draw you? I have noticed that you were unwilling.'

'I am not beautiful.'

'No. But you have power. Your anger has power, and you have power yourself, beyond that.'

She had the idea, then, over the weeks and months when he visited from time to time and sketched her, and Concepción, or ate the *alioli* and supped her red peppers and raisins, praising the flavours, that he would make her heroic, a kind of goddess wielding spit and carving knife instead of spear and sword. She found herself posing, saw him noting the posing, and tried to desist. His interest in the materials of her art did indeed fire her own interest in them. She excelled herself, trying new combinations for him, offering new juices, frothing new possets. Concepción was afraid that the girl would fall in love with the artist, but in some unobtrusively clever way he avoided that. His slit stare, his compressed look of concentration, were the opposite of erotic. He talked to the girl as though she were a colleague, a partner in the mystery of his trade, and this, Concepción saw without wholly knowing that she saw it, gave Dolores a dignity, a presence, that amorous attentions would not have done. He did not show the women the sketches of themselves, though he gave them small drawings of heads of garlic and long capsicum to take to their rooms. And when, finally, the painting of *Christ in the House of Martha and Mary* was finished, he invited both women to come and look at it in his studio. He seemed, for the first time, worried about their reaction.

When they saw the painting, Concepción drew in her breath. There they both were, in the foreground at the left. She herself was admonishing the girl, pointing with a raised finger to the small scene at the top right-hand corner of the painting – was it through a window, or over a sill, or was it an image of an image on a wall? it was not clear – where Christ addressed the holy staring woman crouched at his feet whilst her sister stood stolidly behind, looking also like Concepción, who had perhaps modelled for her from another angle. But the light hit four things – the silvery fish, so recently dead that they were still bright-eyed, the solid white gleam of the eggs, emitting light, the heads of garlic, half-peeled and life-like, and the sulky, fleshy, furiously frowning face of the girl, above her fat red arms in their brown stuff sleeves. He had immortalised her ugliness, Concepción thought, she would never forgive him. She was used to paintings of patient and ethereal Madonnas. This was living flesh, in a turmoil of watchful discontent. She said, 'Look how real the eyes of the fishes are,' and her voice trailed foolishly away, as she and the painter watched the live Dolores watch her image.

She stood and stared. She stared. The painter shifted from foot to foot. Then she said, 'Oh yes, I see what you saw, how very strange.' She said, 'How very strange, to have been looked at so intently.' And then she began to laugh. When she laughed, all the down-drooping lines of cheek and lip moved up and apart. The knit brows sprang apart, the eyes shone with amusement, the young voice pealed out. The momentary coincidence between image and woman vanished, as though the rage was still and eternal in the painting and the woman was released into time. The laughter was infectious, as laughter is; after a moment Concepción, and then the painter, joined in. He produced wine, and the women uncovered the offering they had brought, spicy tortilla and salad greens. They sat down and ate together.